DANDELION MAN

the four loves

W. M. J. Kreucher

This book is a work of fiction. Names, characters, places, and incidents either are products of the author's imagination or used fictitiously. Any resemblance to actual persons, living or dead, events, or locales is entirely coincidental.

W. M. J. Kreucher
Visit my website at walt.kreucher.net

Printed in the United States of America

First Printing: June 2012
dandelion man press
Seventh Edition June 2026

ISBN: 979-8-8692-6423-7

You see how easily we fit together,
as if God's own hand had cradled only us.

—ROD MCKUEN

To my wife Dianne. Thank you for loving me unconditionally.

ACKNOWLEDGEMENT

When you are sorrowful, look again in your heart, and you shall see that in truth you are weeping for that which has been your delight.
—Khalil Gibran

I gratefully acknowledge the assistance and inspiration provided by my son, Benjamin, a gifted novelist. His knowledge and creative spark have led me to venture into the uncharted territory of creative writing. I am also grateful to my loving wife Dianne for her support and patience in listening to my incessant ramblings as I bounced back and forth between reality and fantasy, writing and researching. I never understood how emotionally draining writing can be until I tried it.

CHAPTER 1

Roses in December

If you reveal your secrets to the wind,
you should not blame the wind for
revealing them to the trees.
—Khalil Gibran

How could I have forgotten you–the touch of your hand–that infectious laugh–that heavenly perfume–memories once indelibly imprinted now melted? In truth, you were a year younger than me. In all other ways, you were years ahead. I remember now. Those days long since dissolved into the mist that is memory.

Slowly, my thoughts turn to you. A once forgotten song heard on the radio triggers a neural response that ignites an image. The flashes, once impossible to suppress, had become less frequent with each passing year. Having watched Dad wrestle with Alzheimer's, the loss of a single memory was cause for concern.

Now the memories were filtering back. Memories tucked away so long ago resurfaced, one triggering another, then another. The crisp morning air heightened my senses. I could recall the exact color and texture of your hair, your eyes, your smile, your perfume. It all came back, you–me–Mike.

Gawd, you were beautiful. I wonder what you're doing this morning. Is it raining where you are? Where is it that you are, anyway? Has it really been thirty-six years since I last saw you?

That final image returned–that angelic face. You, dressed in white bridal silk, walking as if ascending into heaven itself to the man you were to spend the rest of your life with. How happy you looked! It was as if you had waited your entire life just for this day–this new life–this man.

I couldn't bring myself to watch the ceremony. It was enough for me to see the finality–the closure of the chapter that was us and the opening of the next chapter–for you, at least.

But why now? Why would you fill my thoughts this morning? What serendipity. There it was, right in front of me in today's newspaper, the obituary for Gerald Zawalski, her father. I scoured the details. Wife Helen, children Gary, Stanley, there it was, Diane McMichael. You were still married to Mike, but then I knew you would be. You had taught me so much about love. The one lesson you reserved for Mike was enduring love.

Could I? Should I? After all these years to be able to see you again, to relive even for a moment our days together; it would be worth it. I remember now. It was your choice–it was always your choice–that struggle of choice. Mike and I only had to live with the choice–and love you.

CHAPTER 2

Old Friends

*You cannot have youth and the knowledge of
it at the same time
– Khalil Gibran*

There are loves we outgrow, loves we lose, and loves we carry — quiet, hidden, stubborn. Some never leave us, even if they've lived a lifetime without us.

My wife, Dianne, and I had played a round of golf that morning in honor of Jerry. He had been a scratch golfer, and he taught me the game. He no doubt smiled down from heaven as I shot a tap-in eagle on the par 5 18th (Lakes 9) at Mystic Creek. When I walked into the Neely-Turowski Funeral Home on Tuesday, June 26th, 2012, I scanned the room and found Dee standing in the back of the chapel in the corner farthest away from the casket. She was talking with a group of people. I walked with my wife to the coffin to say a prayer for her father. Inside the casket was a sleeve of Titleist PRO V1 golf balls and a racing form. His two favorite pastimes. I finished my prayer and waited to speak with Helen. I thought about the first time I met Jerry. He threatened to shoot me if I so much as laid a finger on his daughter. But I loved him. He gave me permission to marry her. He told me so at Gary's wedding, when I was barely nineteen and trembling at the thought.

"You probably don't remember me, but I went to grade school with Gary and I dated one of your daughters. My name is Walt Kreft." I grasped Helen's hands with both of mine.

"Oh my God, Wally Kreft, of course I remember you. Dated one of my daughters indeed. I thought you were going to marry her." Mrs. Z admonished.

I chuckled, a blush covering my face.

Helen turned to Dianne and said, "Sorry."

I introduced Dianne to Helen

"So, another Diane?" Helen smiled.

"Yes, and she's Polish. Hey, when you find a good thing, you have to stick with it," I responded, knowing what Helen meant.

We chatted about things, and Helen mentioned she heard I was doing very well, and I nodded. I never asked how she heard or what all she heard. She mentioned that she and her daughters were talking about me the other day and were wondering if I would show up. We parted as she had other guests who wanted to say hello and express condolences.

As I moved to the back of the chapel, I overheard Michele talking, and I recognized her, so I went up and said hello. We talked about her life (she is married to a doctor now and living in the Tampa area, where she teaches Christian education K-8). She misses Michigan and wants to move back someday.

Helen walked by and placed her hand on my arm. "I can't believe you came," she smiled.

"Your mother is so funny. I'm glad to see she's holding up so well today." I replied to Michele as her mother walked out of the room.

Michele asked if I had spoken with her sister yet, and I shook my head "no, not yet." I looked around to see if I could locate Dee, but did not. Everyone began sitting for the beginning of the prayer service.

Dianne and I sat in the penultimate row, and the Reverend Jarosław Piłus, pastor at St. Suzanne's, led us in the rosary. Michele and Dee sat directly behind us. Michele sat behind me, Dee behind Dianne. I don't think they saw us when they chose their seats, but Michele might have chosen them on purpose. Dee was dressed in a beautiful white, red, and black dress from White House/Black Market. She wore a red sweater over the dress. I recognized the outfit from an earlier shopping trip with Dianne. I liked the dress when I saw it in the store and liked it even more when I saw Dee wearing it. Even in her grieving, she was beautiful.

During the eulogy, Michele related a story about the kindness of her father and his giving nature; how she wished as a child that he would not give so much to charity, to the Catholic Church, how she wished for a new pair of new shoes as a little girl, how important it was to her father that he return to God what was His.

After we finished the rosary and the eulogy, Michele got up and walked away. I stood and walked over to Dee. "Hello Dee, it's so good to see you again." I hugged her and kissed her cheek.

"I miss you," I whispered. Dee looked up. I leaned in, aiming for her forehead like I had on our first date—but at the last second, she closed her eyes and tilted her head as if to kiss me on the lips, and I clumsily bumped into her glasses.

"Oops, I'm sorry. I was just being silly." Embarrassed by my clumsiness, I pulled away and looked into her eyes as she straightened her glasses. "Oh! You don't remember me, do you?" Disappointment leaked from the corner of my eye. The move to kiss me was instinct, not recognition.

"I am trying real hard," Dee replied, staring at my face for a spark of recognition as she readjusted her glasses.

"I'm Wally Kreft," I said with a thin, tight-lipped smile.

"Oh my God, come here," Dee said, her face lighting up as she pulled me close. She began crying uncontrollably, tears of comfort. I could feel her body pulsate with each sob. It was all I could do not to cry myself. I had to tell myself not to say what was in my heart. When I hugged Dee, her perfume reminded me of our first date — the scent of her perfume, Heaven Sent, that night long ago lingered in my senses. I remember standing on the porch outside her house that first night, just before her 16th birthday, afraid to kiss her goodnight. She was so beautiful.

"You have no idea how many times I have thought about you," she whispered in my ear as I hugged her, patted her gently on the back, stroked her hair, kissed her on the cheek, repeatedly.

"I know. And I have thought of you often, too. And yes, I still love you." I said that last part before I could catch myself. Dee still held a special place in my heart.

As Dee pulled away, she looked into my eyes for something. She smiled and started talking, teasing, and patting me on the side of my right leg. Embarrassed to have her touching me so affectionately, I brushed her left hand away with the back of my right hand.

"Dee, I want you to meet someone," I said as I pulled back slightly, reaching over and grabbing Dianne's hand to bring her closer so that I could introduce my two loves. Dee began crying again, tears of joy, I think. Not knowing exactly what to do, I looked at my wife and shrugged my shoulders as if to say, what did I say wrong? Dianne motioned with her head for me to hug Dee again.

"I am so sorry, Dee. I didn't mean to upset you or make you sad." I stroked her hair with my left hand, patted her back with my right, and kissed her repeatedly on the cheek. I continued to hold her tightly until she stopped crying, at least a little. After I broke away the second time, I introduced my two loves to each other.

"It's not sadness, it's just emotion," she said in response to my comment as she smiled sweetly, wiping the tears from her eyes.

"Dee, I would like you to meet my wife. Dianne Kreft, meet Diane McMichael." Even now that name seems wrong, so foreign. I almost said Zawalski.

Diane held out her hand.

"I'm sorry, but I have to hug you," Dianne said almost tearfully.

"I am so glad you came. We never really got the chance to say goodbye... We were both young and stupid." Dee paused and looked at me. I said nothing, embarrassed that my first love would say such a thing now after all these years in front of my wife.

"I can't believe it. I cried at my wedding and I'm crying now."

"I remember your wedding." I wanted to continue, but she interrupted.

"I still have the frying pan you gave me." Dee smiled, reaching out to touch my hand.

"I remember your wedding," I repeated, picking up on the thought I wanted to start. "To this day, I consider you one of the three most beautiful brides I have ever seen," I said, my voice straining to choke back the tears.

"He is such a sweet talker," Dianne smiled at Dee.

"And I know who is number one," Dee replied, reaching for Dianne's hand. I whispered a thank you as Dee hugged Dianne.

We talked about our lives, how she worked as a senior executive at Johnson & Johnson until the 1990s, when she had her little girl.

"Dee, there is nothing I would rather do than stand here and talk with you all night, but you have other people who are waiting patiently to speak with you, so I will leave you to your responsibilities." I leaned in and kissed her one last time on the cheek.

"I want to say a quick hello to Mike before I leave."

I walked over and reached my hand into the small crowd around Mike; Corinne, their daughter, was standing nearby.

"Hello, Mike."

"Walt Kreft," I added in response to the puzzled look on his face. A look of shock replaced the puzzled look. I smiled as I walked out of the room hand in hand with my wife.

As I walked out, Dee's voice stayed with me. Not the words, but the way she said my name. As if she had always kept a small part of me with her. Some loves don't end. They just wait quietly — for a funeral, or a word, or a name said softly enough to open old doors.

~

I drove home that evening with Dianne silent beside me, the streetlights painting stripes across the dashboard. She reached over and took my hand, and I squeezed back, grateful for her steady presence. But my mind kept drifting to the corner of that funeral home, to the smell of Heaven Sent, to the way Dee's body had shaken with sobs against my chest.

That night I slept poorly, waking at intervals with fragments of images I couldn't quite hold onto. The alarm clock read 3:47 when I finally gave up and went downstairs to make coffee. I sat in the dark kitchen, staring at the black window, and found myself thinking not of the funeral home or the church service that awaited us in the morning, but of a porch swing. A September night. The particular way the crickets had sounded in Rouge Park, and how afraid I'd been to kiss a girl who was almost sixteen.

The memories came unbidden in the days that followed, filtering back like sediment rising in a stream. I'd be shaving and suddenly recall the way Dee laughed when I beat her at ping-pong. Driving to the store, I'd remember her mother's voice calling us inside for dinner. Each recollection arrived complete and unexpected - a scent, a phrase, the particular quality of afternoon light through her kitchen window - until the past began to feel more vivid than the present.

By the time we returned to Saint Suzanne's for the funeral Mass, I was already living in two timelines at once. The church had changed in forty years, but my memories of it had not.

~

The following day, my wife and I went to Saint Suzanne's for the Mass of the Resurrection. I had mixed emotions, as I usually do at funerals, more so today. As Dianne and I walked up to the front door, I met Matt, his wife, and their young daughter. I stopped and introduced myself and my wife, offered my condolences, then stooped to speak with the little girl. She wore a sad expression, or perhaps it was a perplexed one. I related the episode of the first funeral of a grandparent I ever attended. "I was about your age when my grandfather died. I thought it was a strange custom; people I didn't know all congregating around my dead grandpa. But you know, we all knew your grandfather in some manner, and we want to pray for him and support the family." Then I pointed to the school next door to the church. "Your father and all your aunts and uncles went to school right there." Then I stood, as my knees were hurting, and I pointed to the southwest. "Your dad and his siblings lived four blocks over there." Then I pointed to the northeast, "and I lived two blocks over there. I went to grade school with your Uncle Gary, and most of my siblings went to school with your aunts and uncles."

I smiled and walked into the narthex. That part of the church still looked like I remembered. It was only when I walked into the nave that things looked different. The blue mosaic behind the altar with a large wooden crucifix hanging from the ceiling was still there as were the two side altars. And the stained-glass windows were as beautiful as I remembered.

But that is where the familiarity ended. The last several pews at the rear of the church had been removed to create a gathering place. That is where they placed the casket for the viewing. Helen was there, surrounded by parishioners, friends and family. Near the front, a large wooden platform took center stage, and on it was a new altar. A Vatican II requirement. The side pews were angled to face the new altar. Not at all what I remembered. As I walked down the center aisle, I met my classmate, Gary. "What are you doing here?" he asked abruptly. I smiled at his surprise. "Just paying my respects. Your father was a good man. I always loved and respected him." As I moved to a pew, I noticed Dee standing near the altar of the Blessed Virgin. Next to her were her husband and her daughter. Dianne asked if I was going to talk to her. "No, I think I will leave her alone this morning." I have regretted that decision as that would be the last time I would ever see her.

My thoughts turned to Dee and to dandelions. A smile came over my face as I relived a happy memory.

The church was filling up as the top of the hour approached. Family and friends are such a comfort. I watched as the next generation, people I had never met, took their place. Some were preoccupied with practicing their readings or just making sure their notes were in a location where they could easily reach them at the appropriate time. Others were chatting with cousins or relatives they hadn't seen in a while, typical family stuff at a time such as this.

The priest, an elderly man with white hair surrounding a balding head who spoke with a Polish accent, was giving last-minute instructions to those who were going to take an active role in the service.

You didn't have to strain to hear the occasional muffled sobs during the service. Not anything out of the ordinary at a funeral. The priest was kind and understanding. In his homily, he spoke of family and grieving:

"In today's Letter of Saint Paul to the Romans, we learn that none of us lives for oneself, and no one dies for one's self. For if we live, it is for the Lord, and if we die, we die for the Lord. Our life is something that is known only by God. Nobody knows all the different facets. Throughout his long life, Jerry loved each of you, some as friends or fellow parishioners, some as relatives, some as children or grandchildren or great grandchildren and one of you as his beloved wife. Each one of you knew him in a different way and loved him uniquely. I can see that love in your faces as I look out into the congregation gathered here today, and I heard it in the stories that you were telling last night at the wake and before Mass this morning as I was walking around. I encourage you to continue to remember him as he enters his eternal home with Our Father."

CHAPTER 3

Cross Country

When you love, you should not think you can direct the course of love, for love, if it finds you worthy, directs your course.
—Khalil Gibran

It was that damn song why I kept that on my playlist, I'll never know. Every time it came on, my thoughts immediately turned to her. But today, I didn't shy away from the memories. Sitting on the patio, staring out into the woods behind the house, I let them wash over me. The smell of the air that morning—cool, faintly smoky, the specific smell of a Detroit fall—was enough. My coffee went cold on the patio table. The neighbor's sprinklers ticked through their rotations, and Dianne was still asleep, but I was seventeen again, with everything still ahead of me and none of it decided yet.

I had dated six girls before her, or at least that is what my seventeen-year-old self would have told you. I was a senior, standing on the edge of the world, and she was a junior, just fifteen, exactly seven days away from sixteen on that first date. In my memory, she was never a child. She was simply the girl who made me understand that the other six had been nothing but rehearsals.

The first time I saw Dee was on a crisp fall afternoon at a cross-country meet in Rouge Park. The course ran along the river, through woods, and across an open field in the shadow of the toboggan hill. We'd grown up with the sight of the Nike missile defense station at its summit, its stark white rockets on their launch pads like thirty-foot sentinels over our childhood sledding runs. But that day, none of us were looking at the missiles.

~

The sight of two girls waiting near the finish line sent a charge through our whole team. We raced up the hills and tore through the woods along the Rouge River, each of us trying to impress the two girls waiting near the finish line. I was at an all-boys Catholic school in the city; the girls attended a new private Catholic high school on the edge of the city. For us, seeing girls at a meet was a rare event, and we weren't about to let the opportunity slip by. After the race, our whole team gathered around them as we headed for the bus, all of us waiting for our teammate Stan to make the introduction.

"How are you getting home?" Stan asked the girls.

"We missed the last bus," Mary Sue replied with a shrug. "We'll have to walk. It's not far, only about a mile."

"We can take you home, can't we, coach?"

"Nope, I'm not allowed to have anyone on the bus except our students' - school rules."

"Ah! That's not fair."

We always called the coach Mr. Depp. He was a scholastic, studying to be a Basilian priest.

"But Mr. Depp, you have to drive right past their street going back to school," I said. I recognized the girls' plaid uniform skirts—they were from Bishop Borgess, my sister's school—and I had a good idea where they lived, since this was my neighborhood.

"You live right off Joy, don't you?" I asked, guessing that this was why they were on the Joy Road bus.

"Yep, on Minock."

"See, coach, it's just a mile down Joy Road. It'll be dark before they get home if they have to walk." I looked at him, and the rest of the team chimed in, a chorus of agreement with me. "Anything could happen."

"All right, get on the bus," he said somewhat reluctantly, motioning for the girls to board the white and blue bus. It was the only time I recall having females on the bus.

The girls cheerfully climbed up the stairs along with the rest of us. They didn't seem to mind the audience of sweaty runners one bit.

Mary Sue sat next to her boyfriend, Stan, and some of the team gathered around her. But Dee, the unattached one, we hoped, drew most of the attention.

For reasons I couldn't explain, Dee chose to sit next to me. Maybe she recognized me from grade school or thought I looked safe. Whatever the reason, I was glad she did, though we were far from alone.

Dee took the aisle seat, but trying to talk to the guys across the aisle meant constantly turning around. 'Here,' she said, and before I could react, she scooted past my knees to the window seat. I leaned back to give her room. Instantly, the team formed a semi-circle around her. The guys in front knelt on their seats, facing us. The ones behind leaned over the seatback, their chins practically resting on our shoulders. We were a dozen sweaty runners, and Dee was at the center of it all.

And we were relentless with the questions and conversation.

"Hi, I'm Wally."

"I'm Bill."

"I'm Władisu."

"I'm Rick."

And so it went. I sorta recognized Dee and asked with a quizzical look on my face, "Do you have a brother, Gary?"

"Yes. Do you know him?" Dee replied.

"I thought so. I went to grade school with him." Now I had an in, I thought. But the questions kept coming from all sides. As we approached the street where the girls would leave us, I got out of my seat and took a few steps towards the front of the bus. "Coach, it's only five more blocks," I shouted.

I sat back down, wanting to ask one last question. Bill asked it for me.

"Aren't you going to ask for her phone number?"

Dee just smiled and winked at me. She pulled out a notebook from her backpack, jotted down her first name, all lowercase with a smiley face above, and her phone number: tiffany six, two, four, one, two. She tore out the small corner of information and handed the scrap of paper to me.

"Thanks," I beamed.

"Please don't call for a few minutes. I still have to walk the rest of the way home."

"Cute," I replied, somewhat sarcastically. She had this sharp, playful edge to her back then. "Hey, Coach, it's the next street ... you can stop anytime," I hollered, tucking the precious piece of information inside the waistband of my uniform shorts. I didn't really need it, though. Once I saw her write it down, the first time I had it memorized the same way I had her face memorized—completely, without trying.

When the bus came to a stop, the girls jumped off, then turned to wave good-by. "Thank you, Coach. We really appreciate the lift home," their voices overlapping just enough to sound rehearsed.

As the girls walked away down the street to their homes, I noticed every boy on the bus had drifted to the same side, faces pressed to the glass, nobody saying a word until the girls disappeared.

"You lucky dog, are you going to call her?" Bill said, punching me in the arm as we returned to our seats.

"If you aren't, can you give me her number? I'll call her for you," Rick chimed in.

"That's okay. I think I can manage it myself." I couldn't wait to get home that night.

Back at school, I changed as fast as I could, grabbed my books, and hitchhiked home. The ride was usually easy to get—alums were always stopping for a kid with a school duffle bag, ready to trade a lift for the latest news from campus.

~

After returning to school, I grabbed my books and headed for home. I wasn't hungry, never was after running and I ate quickly, then went to my room to finish my homework. I finished my homework around eight-thirty and agonized for another twenty minutes before forcing myself to act. I went down to the basement, the only place to find a scrap of privacy with six siblings, and dialed.

When I retrieved the scrap of paper from my pocket, the writing was blurred from sweat. It didn't matter. I had been reciting it over and over in my head as I mentally practiced what I would say, depending on who actually answered the phone.

"Hello," Dee said, picking up the phone on the second ring. She must have been sitting nearby, expecting the call. I don't think she wanted to risk her father picking up the phone first.

"Hi, it's Wally, remember me? I met you earlier today at the cross-country meet." Dee answered, and a wave of relief washed over me. I wouldn't have to make small talk with a parent I'd never met.

"Wally? Wally? Which one were you?" she teased.

"I was the one sitting next to you on the ride home. You gave me your phone number," I replied, wondering why she couldn't place me so soon after our meeting.

"Oh yes, I remember now, the funny-looking one with the glasses."

"Yeah, that's me, I guess," thinking this was a mistake. "I sorta wanted to see you again. We didn't really get a chance to talk much on the bus. Would you like to go see a movie or something this weekend?"

"Sure, what's playing?" she responded in a voice that was lighter than I expected, and I found myself wanting to hear it again.

I didn't have a clue. I hadn't planned that far ahead and didn't know what to say next, but I was already feeling better about calling.

"Ummm, I'm not sure, but we should be able to find something we both would enjoy."

"Sounds good."

"Great! Well, I'll see you on Saturday. I'll call you in the afternoon and we can decide on the movie and the time."

I hung up the phone, ran upstairs and grabbed the newspaper to find the local movie guide for that weekend. Funny Girl opened that week, and I thought it would be good first-date material. It was.

I arrived early on Saturday, about six thirty, to pick up Dee. Reaching the top of the stairs, I rang the bell.

Jerry, her father, greeted me through the screen. It was the one and only time he answered the door when I came over. I think he knew his little girl was going out with a new fella and he wanted to get a good look at me.

"Well, what do you want?" came the gruff response through the screen door. I was only about five foot six or seven and I couldn't have weighed one hundred twenty pounds with my pockets full of rocks. Her father towered over me, one hand braced against the doorframe, the other on the door itself, as if he needed to hold the house back from swallowing me whole.

Jerry was a year past his fortieth birthday when I first met him, almost ten years younger than my father. He was tall and athletically built, a blue-collar type who looked like he'd worked hard all his life, maybe in construction. I would learn later that a deep kindness ran beneath that tough exterior, but that night, all I saw was the man guarding the door.

"I am here to pick up your daughter, sir," I politely said, looking up at him with a smile. I had gone out with enough girls to know this routine, and Jerry was playing his part to perfection.

"Which one? I have three?"

"Diane," I stammered, not knowing just how old the other girls were or even who they were. I hadn't yet met the rest of the family, so I didn't realize that he was teasing me, as Michele was probably twelve or thirteen at the time and Paulette wasn't even in double digits.

"Well, don't just stand there. Come on in." A hint of a smile crossed his face.

And just like that, he held the door open for me. I was in. He closed the door behind me and turned around slowly.

"Who are you anyway? Do I know you?"

"I'm not sure. You might. I went to grade school with Gary and I live just the other side of Saint Suzanne's. You may have seen me at church," I added details, hoping to persuade him I was an acceptable date for his little girl.

"I guess it'll be okay for you to date my daughter."

Jerry turned towards me and stood as close as he could. I swear he was standing in my shoes. He put on his best stern father's face. He tapped his strong finger straight into my chest and said, "but remember this, I have a shotgun in the basement and if you so much as lay a finger on her I will come after you."

"Oh, Jerry, stop it. You'll frighten the poor boy," Helen said, drifting into the living room with a practiced roll of her eyes.

I wasn't frightened by his actions. On the contrary, I felt a strange sense of respect. He loved his daughter enough to protect her, and by letting me date her, he was entrusting me with the most precious gift he possessed.

"Hi, I'm Diane's mother. You can call me Mrs. Z."

I liked her instantly. "Good evening, Mrs. Z. Is Dee ready yet?"

"No, but she should be down shortly. We can talk until she has finished getting dressed. I want to get to know you."

I sat on the edge of the couch, while Jerry retreated into the shadows of the hallway.

"Oh, no you don't, Mom!"

The voice came from the top of the stairs—light, melodic, and full of a fifteen-year-old's indignant fire. Then she appeared.

Dee didn't so much walk down the stairs as bounce down them, light on her feet with an easy, carefree energy that made her seem almost weightless. She was the sort of girl who could hop onto a porch railing without making it groan, all coltish grace and youthful confidence. Barely five-foot-four, she had the fresh-faced, gamine charm that made you think of Sandra Dee in Gidget—bright-eyed, sunlit, and brimming with optimism. She still carried the slender, almost girlish figure of someone who hadn't quite crossed the threshold into womanhood, and there was something disarmingly wholesome about her, as if the world had yet to convince her to be anything other than herself. I thought she was the most beautiful girl I had ever seen, in a way that made me feel I had never really looked at anyone before.

I sprang to my feet. "Hello, Dee."

"Hi. I heard you already met my dad." Her light ashen hair was cut to the jawline, perfectly framing those champagne-colored eyes that held a permanent, mischievous twinkle.

"Yes, I like him," I said, finally finding my breath. "He seems protective of his baby girl."

"Yeah, he means well," she laughed—and it was that laugh, airy and infectious, that made me realize I wasn't just on a date. It was the beginning of something. "And I don't think he would really shoot you."

"Well," I grinned, "that's good to know."

"Ready to go?" I asked, looking forward to our evening adventure.

"Sure, let's get out of here before my mother asks you any more questions," Dee smiled at her mom.

"Now don't stay out too late, you two. You know she has a curfew at midnight," Mrs. Z said, wagging her finger at me as we walked towards the door.

"Oh, I will have her home before then." I thought to myself that my curfew was even earlier than Dee's, but I didn't let on, fearing that Dee's curfew would be adjusted accordingly.

Funny Girl proved to be everything I could have hoped for on that first date. We laughed, and at least I cried. At some point I had reached over and took Dee's hand and held it for most of the movie even though the position of the armrest between us began cutting off the circulation in my arm after a while. During one of the poignant parts, I think Dee noticed the tear in my eye because she squeezed my hand. A simple pressure, but I felt it all the way up my arm. In the dark of the theater, holding her hand, I felt a certainty settle in my chest. There was no turning back.

We stopped at the local McDonald's on the way home. I'd worked there the previous summer, and the manager still gave me free fries whenever I came by. Over a shared order of those fries, we talked, and I found myself learning the shape of her life, piece by piece.

We sat in the car in front of her house, talking until we ran out of excuses to stay. We talked about little things and nothing at all. She told me about her siblings, her spot on the softball team, and how she loved the color of her house. It was just a collection of small facts, but I listened, relishing the smile in her voice.

As curfew approached, I got out of the car and walked around to open the door for her. We walked hand in hand across the street and up the walkway to her door, neither one wanting the night to end.

As we quietly made our way up to the porch, I kept thinking, oh boy, now what? Do I kiss her? Is she expecting a kiss? Is it too soon? Will she be offended that I am trying to put the moves on her? A thousand divergent thoughts raced through my brain in the fifty feet up the walk to the steps. It was an endless journey to a destination that couldn't come quick enough.

At the top of the stairs, we stood under the porch light in front of her door as she fiddled with her keys, looking down at them.

The moment of truth—I had to make a decision.

Dee exuded a sweetness and innocence that was intoxicating. Already, I was addicted. Her soft eyes glanced downward, then back to me, then back to the keys she caressed in her delicate hand. I didn't want to spoil that innocence with a mere kiss. Should I take the chance? If I don't, will I ever get another? Would her brother beat me up? Would her dad really shoot me?

Something clicked in my mind—the timid look on her face, the almost theatrical warning from her father. Looking at her, a thought surfaced, more of a hope than a certainty: maybe this was her first real date. Maybe she'd never been kissed. I glanced toward the front window, half-expecting to see her parents peeking through the curtains. My mind raced. A real kiss felt like too much, too soon. But doing nothing felt worse, like an admission I was only a friend. I desperately wanted a second date and couldn't risk screwing this up.

I reached out and put one hand on each side of her face. Dee closed her eyes, took a deep breath, tilted her head to the right, and leaned forward. The blush on her cheek felt warm in my hands. My heart pounded, longing for her rose lips. The scent of Dee's floral perfume mingled with the faint aroma of freshly cut grass. As I leaned in, then paused, Dee's breath hitched ever so slightly.

Instead of pressing my lips to hers, I kissed her forehead. It felt right. Safer.

When I pulled back, she exhaled softly. The kiss must have startled Dee. Her eyes popped wide open. She gave me this look that said, oh no you didn't just give me my first kiss on the forehead. Then, a calm, gentle expression washed over her face. She didn't retreat; instead, she reached out with her right hand and cradled my chin. Her thumb stroked my cheek. Her delicate hand guided my lips to hers. It was the sweetest, most memorable kiss I had ever experienced in my young life. That first kiss was a sip from the cup of what might be. It joined my soul with hers to create a third soul, 'us'. I was in heaven. God, did I love that girl.

"I had a great time tonight," I choked out. "May I call you again?"

"You'd better. I don't let just any boy kiss me on the forehead."

That forehead kiss became a running joke. Dee told all her girlfriends, and within a week the story had made its way through every lunch table and locker room in her high school, eventually getting back to my sister. 'Girls get kissed on the forehead by their fathers, not their boyfriends,' my sister admonished me. They all teased me mercilessly about it for the next two and a half years. In retrospect, they were right.

~

I'd gone out with two other girls the week before. They were fantastic, good-looking, fun. But after that night with Dee, somehow, none of them mattered anymore.

All I could think about was Dee. The aroma of her perfume, Heaven Sent, lingered on my shirt and clung to the air above the seat where she sat just moments before. The perfume was aptly named. It was an intoxicating fragrance. One part innocence, one part angel, one part mischief.

I enjoyed being with the other two girls, but the feeling was simple friendship. With Dee, it was different from the very beginning. We connected emotionally right from the start.

I'd never been a skilled conversationalist, always more comfortable listening than talking. With Dee, I could listen for hours on end. We talked frequently on the phone and dated on the weekends.

For our second date, I took her to a coffeehouse near Wayne State called the Snug. I'd been there before with friends. It was next to a bar called the Traffic Jam, and I was so nervous I led us into the wrong door.

We came at the building from a different direction that night. When I saw the door, I confidently pulled it open and ushered everyone inside. Then I saw the sign saying that this was the Traffic Jam and that the Snug was around the corner. 'Wait,' I thought, 'that can't be right.' I knew this was the right building. Dee leaned in close. 'What's that sign about?' she whispered. 'It's a joke,' I said, maybe a little too quickly. 'Ignore it.' We sat at the bar, but the feeling of wrongness grew—the taps were unfamiliar, the bartender. He approached us, and I just looked at Dee. She was already smiling, that patient, knowing look on her face. 'Wrong place,' I mumbled, and she squeezed my hand as we got up to leave.

I had had a long day and, on the ride home, I kept nodding off with my head resting on Dee's shoulder. We were double-dating with some friends that evening, and Dee and I were in the back seat. The song

"Hey, Jude" by the Beatles came on the radio and Dee began singing softly to me. Without hesitating, I said to her "You have a great voice; you should be in a choir."

I regretted it the moment the words came out of my mouth. From the front seat, Denise started laughing—not a polite chuckle, but a low, knowing sound that made the back of my neck burn. It was the kind of laugh that had a history behind it, and I knew exactly which story she was remembering.

Dee asked, "What's so funny?" oblivious to the unstated joke.

"Oh, nothing," Denise chuckled. "It's just that I thought I had heard that comment somewhere before."

Dee turned to me and said sternly but also teasingly, "So, you are confusing me with one of your other girlfriends, are you? You had better learn to keep us straight if you want to continue to go out with me."

I felt a hot flush creep up my neck.

"Thanks, Denise. You're a big help."

Before I kissed Dee goodnight, I had to clear the air. 'That other girl,' I started, 'the one in the choir... I'm not seeing her anymore. I'm not seeing anyone else.' The words felt heavy, important. I needed her to know she was special to me, but I didn't feel it was my place to ask for the same in return. I just watched her, waiting. She didn't say anything, but the look she gave me felt like an answer. For now, it was enough.

I remember the time she was invited to be in the local qualifying pageant for Miss Teen Michigan.

It made sense that Dee was invited. She had the easy confidence of a team captain—she led her high school softball team—and the grace of the talented dancer she was. In the swimsuit competition, she walked with a confidence that made the other girls seem like they were just playing dress-up. But where she really shined, the place she was entirely herself, was in the talent portion of the evening.

Her talent was multifaceted: a pen and ink sketch, a dress she made, and a story about a teenage girl who gets pregnant. She started with a joke that made the whole room of nervous parents laugh, but by the end, when her character had to make an impossible choice, a quiet fell over the auditorium. When she finished, the applause was thunderous; people were on their feet. It was a stark contrast to the polite clapping for the other contestants, including the girl who eventually won by stumbling through a patriotic speech. Dee's story was too honest for the judges, but as we exited the auditorium, she was the only one anyone was talking about. Countless questioned her placement as first alternate rather than winner.

The world outside our small orbit felt like it was changing just as fast. The Beatles, our soundtrack for everything, played their last live gig together. On my birthday, they started recording Abbey Road, but you could already hear things were different. While Armstrong was taking his first steps on the moon and someone in a lab was quietly launching the internet, Dee was on a stage telling a story that was too honest for the judges. Watching her, I felt like the rest of the world was still catching up.

CHAPTER 4

Games People Play

*In the sweetness of friendship, let there be
laughter, and sharing of pleasures. For in the
dew of little things, does the heart find its
morning and is refreshed.*
—Khalil Gibran

All this was before the personal computer age set in. We had no video
games to play or DVDs we could watch. If the show we wanted to see
wasn't on TV at the time, we watched what was on or we did something
else. It was not unusual for me to just drive the mile or so over to see
Dee so we could spend time together. I enjoyed her company.
Sometimes we just sat and talked.

I would often talk with Mrs. Z while I waited for Dee to come down
from her room. I enjoyed our talks, and I think her mother did as well.
More often than not, we would discuss an issue of the day or just

philosophize about the color of the sky. It simply didn't matter what the topic was. Nor did it matter which side of the debate we chose, as frequently we would change sides during the discussion, often multiple times in the same conversation. It drove Dee mad.

"Don't you know you just switched sides?" She would say to me in disgust, listening to our conversations but not actively taking part.

"Yes, we're just having some fun. It's my way of communicating with your mother. I like her and enjoy her company. She's a good person," I would say, shrugging my shoulders as if to say I wasn't trying to be argumentative.

"I don't understand you sometimes. How can you like a person old enough to be your mother?"

There are different kinds of liking someone, I thought to myself.

"Well, mothers are people, too. And they were once young, same as you. One day you will be a mother, and I'm sure you will want to get to know your children's companions. What they think, who they are."

"Well, I am not going to be a mother then. I couldn't stand all the arguing," she said, not wanting to think about the possibility of having children of her own.

"We're not arguing. We're just having a conversation," I said calmly, not wanting to get into an argument with Dee.

"Ugh!"

"Come on, we better go before I get you mad. Good bye, Mrs. Z," I smiled. "Nice talking with you."

"Good to talk with you, too. Remember her curfew," Helen called as we were walking out the door.

"You know I will," I shouted back from the porch as I closed the front door.

Sometimes, instead of leaving, we went to the basement where the family had a ping-pong table.

"Mom, Wally and I are going downstairs to play ping-pong. Is that okay?"

"Sure, but I will listen at the kitchen door and I had better hear that ball bouncing back and forth. I don't want you two sneaking down there just to kiss," she would tease.

"Oh, Mother, really." This sort of teasing from her mother embarrassed Dee.

And play ping-pong we did. At least sometimes.

After playing for a while, I would put my paddle down on the table and walk over to where Dee was standing. I would grab her hand and hold her paddle behind her back, then grab her other wrist and bring it around to meet the first hand behind her, hold her close and begin kissing. I couldn't help myself. I just wanted to be near her, to touch her. Together, we would move over to the couch in the basement and continue kissing. It wasn't long before we heard Mrs. Z hollering down the staircase.

"I don't hear that ball bouncing. Are you sure you two are still playing ping-pong?"

"Yes, Mother, the ball just went under the couch and we are trying to find it," Dee said in a little white lie.

"Okay, but you'd better hurry. I want to hear that ball bouncing again, and soon."

Helen didn't mind a little kissing; she just liked to tease.

"Yes, Mother, we will get back to playing table tennis right away." Dee grabbed my face and pulled it towards hers so we could continue kissing.

That is when I learned the difference between ping-pong and table tennis. When Dee wanted to kiss, she would suggest we play table-tennis. When she wanted to play the game involving the paddles and a ball, it was ping-pong. Eventually, I learned the rules to both and enjoyed both immensely.

Charades was another favorite of Dee's. But we only played it with groups of friends. Dee and Mary Sue had a distinctive style of play and could almost read each other's thoughts. They were not above bringing up private jokes from time to time during the games, usually when they were growing tired of playing and wanted to do something else or were feeling frisky.

The first time I saw her act out one of these private jokes as a clue, we were playing mixed partners. Dee and I were a team, and she was giving the clue to Mary Sue and me to see which team would get the clue first.

I was usually reasonably good at the game, but this time, I had no idea what Dee was trying to convey.

Dee placed her forefingers together in front of her body and started moving them apart, forming an imaginary object. She stopped when her fingers were about shoulder-width apart. Then she moved them down toward the floor about two feet, then back toward each other until they touched.

"TV show!" we shouted together, recognizing the category.

Dee touched her nose, indicating we were correct.

Dee placed four fingers in the air.

"Four words."

She tapped her nose again.

Then she did something that shocked me. She was sitting on a chair opposite me, and she spread her legs wide apart. She was wearing jeans, but I thought *this is curious. Why would she do that*?

"Oh, Dee, stop that and give us a clue."

She did it again, this time more vigorously.

Mary Sue started cracking up.

"Come on, Dee, you have to give clues or we'll never guess it before time expires."

Mary Sue and Dee, at this point, were laughing hysterically. There was no hope for an additional clue.

Finally, Mary Sue composed herself enough to shout out the answer.

"Leave it to Beaver"

Dee tapped her nose and fell off her chair, laughing.

"Okay, if you two are going to play that way, we're done," I said. I am not sure why I was embarrassed to see the clue acted out in that manner, but I was. I had to admit, though, that the clue was a good one—albeit kind of gross to see your girlfriend do that in public, even if it was just in front of our friends.

~

The house where Dee grew up was a colonial-style home. With seven kids, they needed the extra space for bedrooms. I never ventured past the living room, dining area, or the kitchen except to go through the kitchen and into the basement. The three girls were forbidden to have boys in the bedrooms, and they were religious about following the rules, although at the time the rule applied mostly to Dee as her sisters were too young to date.

The outside of the house was covered in powder blue asphalt shingles, as was popular at the time (the shingles, not the color). What stood out were the pink shutters hanging on either side of the front windows. There was no mistaking the house. Even first-time guests did not need the address to find the house; you just needed the street and the description. People could pick out the house from a block away with its unique color scheme. I used to tease Dee about it, but it didn't faze her one bit. She loved the house and the colors.

"Pink for the girls, blue for the boys," she would tell me. "It's the perfect family home. The only thing wrong is that hideous red and yellow fire hydrant out front. I really wish *somebody* would come by and paint it to match the house," she said with that devilish look in her eyes only she could manage.

I knew from the emphasis she placed on the word that she wanted me to be that someone.

"Well, they would have to get matching paint and I am not sure they make those colors anymore, or where anyone could find them," I said, hoping to get off the topic.

"Not a problem, we have a can of each color in the garage," she volunteered, trying to be helpful.

"You're the artist. Why don't you paint it?" I said, still trying to avoid being trapped into this random act of vandalism.

"Are you kidding? If my dad ever found out I did that I would get a lickin' for sure. No, it's better if I have some plausible deniability."

"Well then, I won't tell you if I am going to do it or not, but just in case can you leave the paint out Friday night?" I said, resigning myself to my fate.

"Sure," Dee replied cheerfully, thankful that I had picked up on the idea and was willing to do the deed for her.

That Friday after I kissed her good night, I met up with my buddy Rick and we returned to the scene of the crime-to-be. We drove over to Dee's neighborhood, and I parked my car down the block so no one would hear the car door shut when we got out.

We quietly walked down the block. It was a warm autumn evening, and the sounds of TV shows and voices could be heard coming from the open windows of the houses we passed. We tried to whisper so we would not attract attention from anyone who happened to be sitting on their porch or looking out a front window. When we reached Dee's house, Rick and I found the two paint cans along with a rag where Dee had left them on the driveway next to the house.

"Great, I forgot paintbrushes and a screwdriver to open the cans," I whispered to Rick. This caper was starting off badly. "Do you have a Swiss Army knife with a screwdriver?" I asked.

"Are you kidding? Why would I carry one of those?"

"Well, how are we going to open these cans?"

"Beats me. Do you have anything metal in your pocket?"

"Just a few coins and my keys and I am afraid of using the keys 'cause if I break the car key we will be stranded and have to walk home."

We grabbed the cans and the rag and walked quietly down to the small strip of grass between the curb and the sidewalk where the fire hydrant was. I shook one can to mix the paint and Rick shook the other.

Grabbing a quarter from my pocket, I tried opening the cans but could not get enough leverage to pry the lid off so I used the side of my car keys to open the cans being careful not to break off the tip stranding me and the car. I found a stick lying on the ground and used it to stir the paint a little more to get the thick pigments that had settled onto the bottom of the can fully mixed, then sat down on the ground next to the hydrant.

I dipped two fingers, pointer and tall man into the paint can and began painting the red parts on the hydrant in the baby blue. Rick set about painting the yellow parts pink, employing the same finger-painting technique. It was great, like we were back in kindergarten again, playing with a three-dimensional canvas, and we were trying our best not to laugh.

We would duck behind a parked car or lie flat in the grass whenever a car drove down the street so as not to be seen. Fortunately, none of the neighbors were out walking their dogs that late at night, so our nocturnal artistry went undetected. They made the hydrant of cast iron, which meant that there were no polished surfaces. The exterior was pockmarked with all kinds of nooks and crannies.

Before long, I was using my entire hand to smooth out the paint, pressing the tip of my finger into each indentation, covering every dip and crevasse in the makeshift canvas with the warm paint that was oozing between my fingers.

We cleaned up as best we could in the dark using the rag, then quietly made our getaway, leaving the once again sealed paint cans behind Dee's house in the backyard. I was careful to clean the paint off my hands so that I would not leave any telltale paint drips inside the car or on the steering wheel.

My artistic adventure was eventually undone when the fire department came by and repainted the hydrant, but it achieved its effect anyway. Dee relished having a matching house and hydrant, if only for a few weeks. And Mrs. Z was polite enough never to ask me about my involvement in the caper. Perhaps she too secretly wanted the hydrant to match the house.

~

That first Christmas we shared together was special. Christmas was always special in our house. With seven children, even if each one of us received two packages, our tiny living room was full of presents under the Christmas tree. By then, the older kids were all working, so we added to the pile with gifts for our younger siblings and Mom and Dad.

Once we reached high school, the neighbor who dressed up as Santa every year would stop bringing presents for us, but we loved to watch the faces of our younger siblings light up when he came through the door on Christmas Eve. He was a right jolly old elf, and one year he actually grew a white beard. All the kids in the neighborhood looked forward to seeing him at Christmas.

Christmas was an opportunity to host the aunts and uncles in our small house, which was always stuffed to the rafters with extended family during the holidays. The grownups ate at the dining room table, and the little kids ate in the kitchen to be near the moms in case they were needed.

The teenagers would get to eat in the basement. By then, Dad had finished the basement, and my brothers and I moved into a bedroom he had partitioned off down there. Dad even added a second bathroom with a shower, which cut the family prep time in half. We would put up an artificial aluminum Christmas tree downstairs for our own little party.

I introduced Dee to everyone that first year, though I doubt she remembered half of them after that initial meeting. She looked so cute with her golden hair, a white blouse and a green velvet skirt—

very Christmassy—my own little Christmas Carol. As much fun as it was to be with extended family at that time of year, it was even more special the first time I brought a girlfriend to a family gathering at the house. In many respects, it was a major milestone, and I was proud to share it with such a special woman.

~

One would have thought that a guy as smart as me would have something memorable in mind come that first Valentine's Day. Oh sure, I had other girlfriends in previous years on that day of lovers, but none of that meant as much as Dee. A romantic card, a heart-shaped box of chocolates — all would have been good choices.

That Friday we drove over to the Raven Gallery, one of our favorite places. Josh White Jr. was performing. The Raven occupied a modest building on Greenfield Road that seated only about 160 people. Paintings by Michigan artists lined the walls. Folding chairs and café tables were arranged close to a tiny stage. The scent of coffee mixed with fresh paint and varnished wood filled the room. Soft lighting focused on the artwork and the stage. It was perfect for quiet conversation between sets. Many soon-to-be famous folk artists began their careers there.

It was on the way home that things took a turn. Sitting in the car in front of Dee's house afterwards, we talked. I had just received my senior class ring and kept playing with it, rotating it around my finger. I wasn't used to wearing jewelry. On the spur of the moment, I took the ring off and slipped it onto Dee's slender ring finger.

A squeal of surprise and delight emanated from her lips. Dee thanked me profusely and repeatedly—giving me kisses all over my face. But I was young and stupid about the ways of love. I began to think about how my mother would react, knowing I had given such an expensive gift to a girl. My mom did not approve of the whole "going steady" thing and would not allow my sisters to do this. It was never specifically mentioned to me, but the more I thought about it, the more I worried I would be in trouble when I got home.

In one of the boneheaded moves of all time, I asked Dee if it would be alright if she only wore it when we were together and would she be willing to give the ring back at the end of each evening together.

"No, thank you. I think you should just keep it yourself until you are ready to give it to me for real." And with that, she took it off her finger and handed it back. What an idiot I was. Looking back on that day, I am surprised that she didn't break up with me on the spot.

~

That same month was the first birthday I celebrated with Dee. I turned eighteen that year and was already accepted to UM, where I would attend in the fall. I thought myself mature at the time, but I was naïve about a great many things. When I applied to college, it never dawned on me they would not accept me so I applied to only one school, the College of Engineering at the University of Michigan. Fortunately for me, I was accepted and began planning for the transition to college life; getting a dorm room, selecting roommates—that sort of thing.

Dee made my birthday special. She baked me a chocolate birthday cake, and we went to a party at a friend's house. Just spending time with her was special, and I was beginning to realize that in six short months I would not be seeing her as often. I treasured every moment we had together.

In April of that year, the Beatles released Old Brown Shoe. I loved that song. It seemed to be written about Dee. I still think of her when I hear it. We were as comfortable together as a favorite pair of old shoes.

CHAPTER 5

Dandelion Man

*that first kiss, to sip from the cup of what
might be, to join his soul with hers, to create a
third soul, 'us'.*
—*W. M. J. Kreft*

Back in the day, there was a board game 'Barbie - Queen of the Prom'. It was popular during the sixties. Dee was my queen, but she would tell you that I was her Poindexter.

"Dee, my senior prom is on May third. Would you like to go with me? The prom is at a country club?" I asked four or five weeks ahead of the event. My sisters had already informed me I couldn't wait until the last minute to ask, even if I was certain Dee would accept.

Dee, in typical coquettish fashion, played coy.

"Mmmm! I don't know," she said, pretending to be thoughtfully contemplating the simple request. "I will have to check my social calendar and ask my mom."

"Well, don't keep me waiting too long. I don't want to miss senior prom, and if you aren't interested, I want to have time to ask another girl." I knew she was just being playful.

"You better not. I'll go. I'll go. But you have to promise to buy me some flowers to match my dress," she said, slapping me on the arm.

That sounded fair.

"What color is your dress going to be?"

"I don't know yet. I'll let you know." Dee hadn't decided on which of the many gowns she had been looking at in the stores she would select.

~

When I called a few weeks later, Dee told me she had made this gorgeous yellow, high-waisted, floor-length gown. I remember it was shiny silk above the waist and more of a satin fabric below the waist. She trimmed it with petite white daisies around the sleeves and at the waistline.

"Remember, you promised to get some flowers that would match. And I want something special—something that all the other girls will look at and envy me for having. Something unique."

Dee really seemed to be hung up on this flower business. But I figured maybe she didn't get flowers that often and she wanted to remember the occasion of her first prom and her first flowers.

I wracked my brain trying to come up with some flower that would be unique, that would really stand out from the ordinary. I asked my mom for suggestions. I even asked my sisters what flowers girls liked. In the end, I drove to the neighborhood florist who had a shop on the corner of Joy and Minock just a few houses from where Dee lived and told the lady behind the counter just what I needed.

"I'd like to order some flowers for prom."

"What day are the flowers for?"

"May third."

The lady behind the counter wrote the information down on her order pad.

"And what color dress will the young lady be wearing?"

"A pale yellow."

"Sounds lovely."

"Yes, I am sure it will be. I was given very specific instructions. No flowers that can be pinned on the dress and it had to be something that was unique. Something that no one else will have."

"Oh, you just leave that to me. We have creative floral arrangers. I am sure we can come up with something that will be special for that young lady of yours. How do you want to pay for this?"

"Cash please." I had no clue that you could pay for something any other way.

"We can do something quite nice for fifteen dollars. Would that be acceptable?"

This being my first time in a florist shop, I didn't know if that was high or if the lady was giving me a deal.

"Sure," I said in a non-committal tone.

"You can pick the flowers up after noon on the third," the florist informed me after I handed her the money.

I drove home, still thinking about the flowers. For days and days, I could not get the instructions from Dee out of my head. On the day of the prom, I picked up my powder blue tux and Dee's flowers and brought them home. I thought the miniature double yellow daffodils intermixed with white baby's breath were beautiful. The lady in the flower shop told me they represented joy and lightheartedness. Dee was sure to love them. I put the flowers in the refrigerator and went outside. I was lying on the grass in the backyard, staring at the sky doing my sky view repeats and thinking when suddenly it came to me. In the neighbor's yard were a few dandelions.

Yellow. Perfect. I would get a second bouquet for this special occasion, I thought, proud of myself for coming up with a unique solution to my dilemma.

There weren't enough dandelions around the yard, so I went back into the house, grabbed the keys to the family station wagon, and told my mom I was going for a short drive.

"What? Now? Don't you have to get ready for your prom?"

"I'll be fine. I have plenty of time, and I won't be gone long."

I drove to the nearby high school, about six blocks away, where they had an enormous field. To my great pleasure, it was covered that afternoon in beautiful yellow dandelions. I selected three dozen of the finest long stem specimens I could find and gathered them into a bouquet. *There, that will look great,* I thought, studying the flowers from every angle.

I drove home and found a yellow ribbon in the closet where we kept the wrapping paper and tied the flowers together, fashioning a bow around the stems with the ribbon, then I put the dandelions in water in the refrigerator next to the real flowers. I didn't want them to wilt prematurely.

As I showered and got dressed, I whistled. I was in a great mood. I was so proud of myself for finally coming up with a unique bouquet that I was certain would match the gown and that no other girl at the prom would have.

I grabbed both bouquets of flowers and headed out the door to pick up Dee.

"See ya, Ma, I'm going now," I shouted as I walked out the door.

"Remember to bring her back for pictures. I want to see her dress."

"Oh, Mom," I said, rather embarrassed at the thought of having to pose for photos.

I drove over to Dee's and walked up to her door with both flowers in the box. I was still whistling a cheery tune as I skipped up the steps in front of her house. I opened the box and took out the yellow daffodil nosegay and placed it on the chair on the front porch, then closed the box and rang the bell.

"My, don't you look handsome," Mrs. Z said, opening the door for me.

"Thank you. Is your daughter ready yet?" I said with a big smile on my face.

"Of course not, but she shouldn't be long. Please sit down."

Taking a seat, I talked with Helen about our plans for the evening. I stood when the scent of Dee's signature perfume reached my nostrils, and I looked towards the hall where Dee entered, dressed in her new gown.

She was beautiful.

I could not believe my eyes. Regretting my decision on the flowers and I put the box behind my back, thinking I could hide it from her. Mrs. Z could see instantly the beauty of her daughter reflected in my adoring eyes.

"Oh, wait, I forgot my camera. I need to get it. I hope I have film and fresh batteries. Don't leave before I get back. I want to take some pictures." She hurried out of the room in search of her camera.

"Are those for me?" Dee asked, noticing the box I was still holding behind my back.

"Yes, but I have to apologize. I know you wanted something special. I didn't realize how long it took to order unique flowers and the shop said they were overly busy today with other prom orders, so I hope these are acceptable," I said, sheepishly handing her the box.

Please don't get mad, please don't get mad, I kept thinking. I wanted to rip the box from her hands, race to the porch and retrieve the real flowers, but it was too late. Dee opened the box.

She took one look inside and started laughing hysterically. She must have laughed for five minutes straight. It was meant to be a joke, but I honestly didn't think it would be that funny. Helen, upon hearing the commotion, came running.

"What's the matter, dear?" Helen asked, thinking something was wrong with her daughter.

Dee was laughing so hard she couldn't talk. She just showed her mom the open box of flowers.

"Oh, you two deserve each other," Helen said, shaking her head and returning to her search for the camera. I didn't understand the comment, but when Dee finally regained her composure, she said, "We must have ordered at the same time from the same florist."

Entirely probable, since the florist was just down the block, I thought.

Dee went to the kitchen to retrieve my boutonniere. I opened the box she handed me and got the joke.

She had purchased the largest chrysanthemum she could find for my boutonniere. It had to be seven inches across, almost as big as my entire face.

"Very funny," I said with a smile. "I guess great minds think alike."

"I don't know about great minds, but we certainly are on the same wavelength. And we know each other's sense of humor."

She went back into the kitchen and brought me my real flower, a white carnation dipped in blue, and I retrieved her nosegay from the porch and handed it to her.

"Thank you, Wally. They're simply beautiful. These are more than I could have imagined or hoped for. I love them." She grabbed my jaw with her free hand, turned my face to the side and kissed me tenderly on the cheek, leaving a pale pink lipstick stain. I didn't wipe off the lipstick.

~

After the obligatory photo session at Dee's, I drove back to my house for another photo shoot. Dee and I met up at my house with our double date partners for the evening, Ken and Pudge. How she got that nickname I'll never know, as she was anything but a pudge. She was about four feet ten inches tall, and she couldn't have weighed eighty-five pounds soaking wet. She had light brown hair, was attractive in an innocent-looking way with a mischievous smile, and I liked her a lot. A year earlier, she had talked me into dating her best friend and teammate on the high school cheerleading team, but it didn't work out. Judy was at least four inches taller than I was. A nice girl with a great personality, a lot of fun to be with. I always got a kick out of seeing Pudge and Judy together. It was like Mutt and Jeff.

The drive north to the country club where the prom was held was interminably long. I thought surely we would fall off the end of the earth before we arrived. I had never been that far from home on a date in my young life. Little did I know that later in life I would live a few miles farther north.

I talked Dee into wearing our "normal people" flowers to the prom. We made the rounds, greeting all my classmates and their dates before sitting down for our dinner. Besides Ken and Pudge, Tom, one of my roommates next year at college, and his date, Mary, were our dinner partners for the evening. After dinner, Dee asked if I would go get our "real" flowers.

"Ken, toss me the keys. I need to get something from the car."

"Okay, but be careful. If the faculty catches you with booze, you may not be allowed to graduate with the class," he said urging caution. He didn't want to be guilty by association if the faculty found any booze at the table.

"Don't worry. It'll be alright."

I went to the car and picked up Dee's dandelion bouquet and my new boutonniere. Returning to the country club, Dee pinned my ginormous flower on the opposite side of my tux from the carnation. Dee picked up her dandelions and asked, "Would you like to dance, kind sir?"

She was a gifted dancer, very graceful. We danced all around the floor, making sure everyone saw our flowers. Some of the girls chuckled—others came up to us to make a comment.

"Oh, how could you do that to such a beautiful young lady?" They scolded.

Dee beamed. "I know. See what I have to put up with. I just don't know what I am going to do with him."

"Oh, you love it and you know it," I whispered in her ear, knowing full well that this was the attention she was seeking.

Dee kissed me on the lips.

Back into heaven.

The band played our song, "My Girl" by the Temptations.

"I got sunshine on a cloudy day. When it's cold outside, I got the month of May. I guess you'd say what can make me feel this way? My girl (my girl, my girl) talkin' 'bout my girl," I sang, looking Dee in the eyes while still swaying back and forth on the dance floor. God, I loved that girl.

Dee smiled at my singing and kissed me again.

Back into heaven.

I had a terrible voice, but I loved to sing. I was in a choir in grade school and whenever we were about to sing before the parents or in church for some special occasion, the choirmaster, the nervous type, would approach me before the performance and say, "now remember to open your mouth wide today, but don't let any sound come out." This continual request embarrassed me, but I always did as he directed.

We closed the country club down that night, not wanting the evening to end. As we strolled to the car, Ken asked, "What time does everyone have to be home?"

Dee was the first to chime in. "Mom said as long as I am home before Dad gets up for breakfast, I would be alright."

"Me too," said Pudge.

"Well, everyone up for going to the submarine races?" I asked hopefully, knowing full well that the girls would agree.

"Sure," came the unanimous reply.

Dee rested her head on my shoulder as Ken began the long drive back into town. I put my arm around her shoulders and held her hand while we rode quietly together. It was one of those peaceful moments that felt small at the time but stayed with me for years.

When Ken made it back into town, he found a quiet spot in Hines Park so we could all talk and enjoy the last part of the evening. Dee and I sat in the back seat while Ken and Pudge took the front bench seat of the old green Dodge Coronet.

We laughed and talked for what felt like only a few minutes, though hours passed. As daylight began to approach, Dee smiled and asked, "Are you ready for one more prom night tradition?"

"I guess," I said, surprised and curious about what she meant.

"I'm wearing something special, and if you can find it, it's yours," she said playfully.

"A scavenger hunt? I'm going to enjoy this."

She guided my hand to the ribbon tied around her leg, beneath the hem of her gown.

"A garter?" I asked.

"Yes," she said. "You may have it."

Dee adjusted her dress so I could reach it more easily while everyone in the car laughed and teased us.

"What are you two doing back there?" Pudge asked over the seat.

"Oh, mind your own business," Dee replied. "Ken, can't you keep that girl busy?"

The garter was handmade—purple silk with white lace trim—and it fit neatly around her leg. Dee was talented with sewing and always had an eye for beautiful details. I carefully slipped it free and held it up proudly.

"I'll treasure this forever," I said.

And I did. When I got my own car, I hung it from the mirror for years as a reminder of a wonderful night and a memory I would never forget.

The next day, most of the senior class went to Kensington Metropolitan Park for a picnic. One last chance for us to see each other, since many of my high school friends were going out of state to college in the fall. A few of the guys volunteered to man the barbecue; the rest of us built a fire and sat around reliving high school memories until it drizzled.

It was a cold, damp day, and we were not dressed for the weather. Dee and I were both shivering before long. The rain put out the fire, but fortunately we had a covered picnic area sheltering us from the rain. There was a concrete floor to keep the mud down and several picnic tables to sit on.

"I'm cold, unbutton your coat," Dee demanded.

I did as she instructed, knowing that by giving her my coat, I was going to be even colder.

She unfastened the snaps on her coat as well. We took our arms out of the sleeves, keeping the coats wrapped around our shoulders. Dee snapped my snaps onto hers in the front and then her snaps onto mine in the back. I had one arm in my outside sleeve away from her body and the other wrapped around her waist inside the jacket. She did the same on the opposite side. This way, we could at least conserve body heat. Dee was always thinking about things like that. When she put her mind to something, she always accomplished her goals, even if it was unconventional.

"Hey, we can't see what your hands are doing under there," Pudge scolded.

"That's none of your business," Dee replied demurely.

We passed that summer lost in love as Peter, Paul and Mary would sing. A girl so sweet that when she smiled, the stars rose in the sky …

I love that song. And how prophetic, little did I know at the time, that I would live out the rest of the lyrics.

I worked two jobs that summer. I needed the extra money for college. During the day, I swept floors in the main powerhouse of the Ford Rouge Plant. It was brutal. There were three large coal-fired multi-floor boilers feeding steam to the turbines in the electric generators. Being the lowest on the seniority list and just a summer temporary employee, I got the job sweeping floors in the turbine room. The turbines ran at a constant, bone-deep thrum that you stopped hearing after a while, until the moment you stepped outside and realized how loud the silence felt. The air carried a heavy, scorched mineral smell that coated the back of your throat, part fireplace, part something older and industrial that no open window could ever fix. Coal ash has a particular smell—not quite smoke, not quite earth—something burnt down past the point of recognizable, and after an hour in that room it lived in your clothes for the rest of the day. There was a sulfurous undertone beneath the ash smell, the kind that made you think of deep underground places, and no amount of sweating it out seemed to push it from your nose. It had to be twenty degrees hotter in there than it was outside, and there was no air circulation. I was popping salt tablets constantly, and I was always soaked in sweat at the end of my shift.

From there, I went home, showered and ate a quick dinner. Then I drove to Butzel Park to work the concession stand at a city owned facility. The park had lighted baseball fields for summer and a lighted outdoor hockey rink in the winter. When I played hockey in high school, that was my home ice. There were always night baseball games at the park during the summer, but I never knew what teams were playing or any of the scores, just some city league games.

The concession stand was in a building between the ball diamonds and the ice rink. Housed within the building were restrooms and a couple of locker rooms that the teams could use. Rick, a classmate of mine, was my co-worker that summer. He was also a member of our cross-country team and had met Dee at that first event. He was always jealous of us and constantly bugging me to let him date Dee. I would tell him he could call her if he wanted, but she would not go out with him. I was confident about that.

Neither Rick nor I were big. We were five feet seven at most and only a hundred twenty-five pounds each, so neither of us was physically intimidating. This was two years after the race riots in Detroit. The park was in a somewhat rough neighborhood, and some teens gave us grief from time to time, nothing serious. Mostly the parents kept the teens in check, but one night a group of teens came up just as we were about to close.

When the games ended, that was our signal to shut down the concession stand for the night. A group of teens wanted some free food, and sometimes we gave them the leftover hot dogs. No big deal, as we just tossed them out at the end of the night anyway. That night we sold our last dog about twenty minutes earlier, so there was nothing left and the teens were not happy.

"Give us some candy instead," they demanded.

"I can't. We have to account for everything except the leftover hot dogs. If anything is missing, it comes out of our paycheck, and we don't get paid much to begin with."

"Well, it's that or we're coming over this counter and we'll get it ourselves." Hawkeye was the leader of the gang. He earned that name because of a corneal ulcer he had in one eye, a souvenir from a previous fight. He had a menacing look, even without the scar on his eye.

"Rick, go out and put the shutters up," I told my partner, nodding my head towards the door. He gave me a dirty look but walked out anyway with the metal shutters while I continued talking to the guys through the open window.

"Now come on. You don't want to do that. If you do, I'll have to call the police (we had a phone in the concession stand) and I won't give you any more free dogs."

"Come on man, let's leave them alone. They're just working stiffs. It's not worth it," someone in the group said and thankfully, they all walked away.

Rick put up the metal shutters, and I locked them in place from the inside. We closed up shop and hurried to our cars, half expecting to be met in the parking lot. We made our escape and drove home, relieved that the ordeal had ended with no further incident.

It was a hot Friday evening, still ninety degrees, even that late at night. I didn't have to work the day shift at my other job on weekends, so I had the next morning off. When I got home, I was still keyed up from the confrontation and decided to go for a run to release the built-up tension. I put on a pair of running shorts, a tee shirt, and my running shoes.

"Mom, I am going out for a run, be back in an hour," I hollered to my mom as I went out the side door of the house. We lived on a corner, so I could get right into the street to begin my run.

"Okay, be careful and watch for cars."

I had called Dee before I left and told her I would stop by in a bit. She lived only a mile south of my house, so it took no time at all to get there. I was running fast and not out for just a casual jog. I needed the release. I arrived at her house and knocked on the side door. Dee answered right away and came outside to greet me.

"Let's sit in the backyard. You look all sweaty." Dee said. She didn't what to hug me or even touch my sweaty body. It was hot, and I had been running hard. We walked into the backyard, and I took my shirt off and sat it on the picnic table, trying to cool down.

"Eeek!" Dee exclaimed in mock horror. "Are you trying to show off your lack of muscles for me?"

"Hey, I'm tough for my size," I said, striking a muscleman pose.

Dee laughed. She grabbed my shirt and raced over to the above-ground pool that was behind her house. It was about four feet deep, big enough for the whole family and many of the neighborhood kids, with a wood deck on one side and a ladder that could be lifted to lock out the little kids from accidentally climbing up and falling into the pool when no one was around. Dee threw my shirt into the middle of the pool.

"You are going to have to go in and get it now," I insisted.

"No, I'm not; it's your shirt. If you want it back, go in and get it yourself." Her innocent smile betrayed her defiant tone. I think she just wanted me to take a quick bath before I got close to her.

I grabbed her around the waist and lifted her into my scrawny arms. As she struggled to escape, I carried her over to the pool and dropped her over the side. She hung onto my neck, but eventually realizing that she could not pull me in, she let go, dove underwater and swam over to retrieve the shirt. She threw it at me, then swam back to the ladder, pausing before she climbed out. Leaning backwards, she dipped her head into the water to pull her hair back against the side of her head. She splashed me and was more than a little perturbed as she climbed out of the pool and down the stairs.

"Walter, Michael, John, Peter."

When your mom uses your first and middle name to call you, you know you are in trouble. Well, Dee not only used my first and middle name but added my confirmation name and threw in one more just to make sure I got the message.

Her jeans were soaked, and so was her tee shirt. We walked to the back of the yard, and I sat on top of the picnic table. I placed my hands on her damp hips as she stood in front of me.

"Sorry. I probably shouldn't have done that. I should have gone in myself to retrieve the shirt. I apologize."

"You'd better," Dee said, wiping some of the water off her hair with the flat of her hand and splashing it in my face.

"I guess I deserved that. Are you mad at me?"

"Yes," she said with a pouty face.

"Come here. How can I make it better? I don't want you mad at me."

I grabbed her around the waist and sat her on my lap, wet jeans and all. I hugged her tightly to my body. She smiled compassionately, and I knew everything would be okay. We kissed affectionately, with Dee perched on my lap. I gently rubbed my finger down the side of her cheek and stroked her wet hair. She was the most beautiful drowned rat I had ever seen.

~

At the end of summer, Dee and I went to Camp Dearborn, just outside of Milford, with some of our friends and their dates for an all-day outing. The camp was a large complex complete with swimming lakes, paddle boats, picnic tables, and even a tent village where families would spend large parts of the summer. After dark, they would close off one of the parking lots and hold dances.

We had ourselves a veritable feast that afternoon. One last fling, you might say. I made the mistake of bringing a large watermelon as my contribution to the menu. Great summer fare, but there was always the problem of discreetly or at least politely disposing of the seeds. Not a problem for Dee. She quickly discovered the perfect way to dispose of them. She spat them at me from across the picnic table. By the end of the meal, I had them all over my face and shirt.

"You'll pay for this, young lady," I said feigning anger.

"Ooooooo! What are you going to do, spank me?" she teased, laughing at the sight of all the seeds covering my face.

"Hmmmm! I'll think of something," I threatened.

After we cleaned up the table and policed the area, I took Dee for a walk around the park. We found a secluded picnic table away from the beach and any other picnickers. Dee wore this adorable baby blue bikini, and I had on navy blue swim trunks and a tee shirt. I sat down on the picnic table and pulled Dee onto my lap.

"What do you think you're doing, Mister?" Dee asked.

"I told you that you would pay for the watermelon seeds. Now you're going to get what you deserve."

Dee looked at me and smiled that innocent smile of hers. I perched her on my lap.

I looked at Dee, perched on my knee like a sun-warmed cat, and everything I'd ever believed about beauty and goodness seemed suddenly true. She had a way of nestling in—her legs folded sideways, her head tipped so I caught the barest glint of her smile, a conspiratorial upturn in her lips—and I wanted to keep her there forever. She examined her hands, waggled her fingers theatrically like a vaudeville magician, then placed them both over her face as if shy, but peeked through the slats. I traced the line of her arm with my own, and with a kind of quiet awe, said, "Have I ever told you I love you, Dee."

She lowered her hands, and for a heartbeat I thought she might turn away, that I'd overstepped, that the spell would break. Instead, she leaned in, her hands on either side of my jaw, and kissed me with a warmth so gentle and certain that it was as if she'd been waiting years for just this moment. My chest filled with lightness, the ridiculous giddiness of first love—so much that I thought I might actually float. Her lips were cold from the watermelon, and she tasted of lake water and the faintest hint of Coppertone. I memorized the taste, thinking I'd need it later, when the world wasn't so perfect.

I thought: This must be what angels feel, if angels ever got to be happy.

I found myself laughing, not at her, but at myself—a helpless laugh, a can-you-believe-how-lucky-I-am laugh. Dee pressed her forehead to mine and regarded me with solemn champagne-colored eyes.

"Was that okay?" I asked, brushing a strand of wet hair from her cheek.

"Oh, more than okay," she said, and then she kissed him again, more insistent this time, her hands drawing me in. I could sense her confidence blooming, the way she'd learned the rules of this new territory and decided she liked them. We knotted ourselves together on the edge of the picnic table, her laughter rippling quick and true. A bee circled lazily near our heads, drawn by the sweetness, but she ignored it, and so did I.

The park around them was loud with the ruckus of other teenagers and the tinny blare of transistor radios, but inside their little bubble all that sound fell away. I told her, barely above a whisper, "I love you, Dee." The words came out like a secret. I didn't expect her to answer in kind—she rarely did—but she kissed the tip of my nose and said, "I know, Wally. I always knew."

I thought of the week ahead: graduation, the looming September of college, the slow drift into lives apart. I tried not to think of it, clinging instead to her damp warmth, the smell of the lake. I wanted this endless, blue-skied day to last forever. When we finally disentangled, she smoothed her hair, fixed her bikini top, and grinned at me with open mischief.

"Let's go find the others," she said, and I nodded, casting one last look at the sunlit spot where we'd made their little memory. I wondered if the grass would remember the shape of our bodies, the echo of our laughter.

We joined our friends at the makeshift dance, Dee's hand tight in mine. For the rest of the evening, whenever our eyes met, there was a shared secret, a private constellation only we could see. Even as the night cooled and the music shifted to slow, sappy songs and the headlines of the day crept back into my mind, I knew: this was the happiest I'd ever been.

We drove home in the darkness, windows down, the air thick with pollen and the ozone tang of coming rain. Dee rested her head on my shoulder, humming along to the radio, her hair drying into a wild, beautiful tangle. I didn't want to let her go, not ever, but I knew, even as I pulled up outside her house and watched her skip inside, that I'd spend the rest of my life chasing that feeling of her on my lap, her lips cold and sweet, her laughter unlocking the world.

~

I loved the sweetness of her lips–the softness of her cheek. It's just that kissing was one way I showed my affection for Dee during our time together. It is what people in love do. To be sure, I showed my affection for her in other ways as well. When we walked together, even for a short distance, we constantly held hands. When we sat with friends, I always made sure we were touching—a hand, the sides of our legs–a toe–perhaps just a finger.

Dee taught me that this physical contact, even in the smallest gesture, was important–it became a necessity for me, almost, you could say, an addiction. I craved the slightest touch from her, and I cherished those moments, reflecting on them when we were separated, always longing for additional contact. To this day, her kisses still linger in a special place in my heart.

~

That summer, the musical Hair was playing downtown at the Fox Theater. Her mother would sometimes work as an usher at the theater and, for this production, management wanted to get some young "hippies" to be the ushers. Helen signed Dee and me up to usher one of the weekend performances, thinking we would at least enjoy the play.

Well, I was anything but a hippie. My high school had strict rules about hair length and a dress code but I figured what the heck I was going up to the University of Michigan in a few months, the founding home of a movement known as Students for a Democratic Society, and I wanted to see what this was all about. SDS dissolved later that year, but some of the members resurrected part of the group into the Weather Underground and another part into the Black Panthers. The latter was a radical group that dug bomb craters on the front lawn of their off-campus house and around campus, symbolizing the destruction US troops were doing in Southeast Asia.

Dee had bought a couple of white tee shirts for us and tie-dyed them. She told me I had to get some bell-bottomed jeans to wear for the event. When I came to her house that evening to pick her up to take her to the theater, she really looked the part. She even made herself a leather headband. Gawd, did she look beautiful! She made a much cuter hippie than I did, that's for sure. I looked more like a geek masquerading as a hippie and felt that way as well. Not her. She could have easily been mistaken for a member of the cast.

We went down to the theater early and received the basic instructions on our jobs and the seating arrangements. I was assigned a row off to the side on the main floor and they stationed Dee in the center of the theater on the other end of the row that separated us. As the orchestra came out to tune up, we hurried everyone to their seats, and I closed the rear doors to the theater. The lights dimmed and the rock music began—powerful rock ... "The Age of Aquarius." I was swaying my shoulders back and forth in time to the music. You couldn't help it. Eventually, some patrons got up and danced in the aisles.

Hmmm, should I go stop them? I thought.

Other patrons, real hippie-looking types, stood up and started climbing over the seats in front of them, moving towards the stage.

Oh, this can't be good. I've got to put a stop to this. The show is about to start. I thought, *how come no one else is rushing up to prevent this?*

Just then, the doors behind me burst open. They had instructed me to close them when the music started, and now they were open again. A rush of hippies stormed through the doors and ran onto the stage. This was the actual start of the performance and all these "patrons" were the cast.

Hair broke new ground in the rock music genre. It was controversial not only for its anti-war theme but also for a scene at the end of Act One where everyone on stage was nude. Mrs. Z had warned us about it.

"And I want you both to close your eyes at the end of Act One. I don't want you looking at all those naked bodies," she instructed us before we headed down to the theater.

I should have known better. She would never have let her little girl or even her little girl's boyfriend see people who were naked on stage. The actors were all wearing tight fitting skin toned full body suits. We enjoyed the performance, and it was eye opening to glimpse the anti-war movement up close—even if it was only a theatrical version of life.

CHAPTER 6

The Four Loves

Life unfolds itself in mysteries ways.
—Khalil Gibran

With Dee there was an almost immediate need on my part to be with her, a delightful preoccupation, and I wanted desperately to give myself to her.

At once she was my friend, my companion. Had she been a man, I would have been friends with her just as quickly as she possessed those qualities that draw a person to her. Her laughter, her wit, her kindness, her thoughtfulness all called to me as none before. I had many friends, but would have forsaken them all just to gain friendship with her. That was not necessary, of course, as she got along famously with all my friends. It was enough that I would have abandoned my life as it existed just to gain this new life with her. I needed her at my side. But I wanted to be more than friends. I wanted to show my affection for her. There was a warm comfortableness in just being with her.

I don't remember there ever being a time when I was not in love with Dee. It was on our first date that I fell in love with her. What a funny phrase, "falling in love." When one falls, doesn't one feel helpless? Isn't falling dangerous? The same applies to love. I appreciated the gift of love she willingly gave me. Even in the ease and ordinariness of our everyday relationship, I had a deep craving just to sit next to her. It was a comfort.

As a test of this gift once, I just sat with her, pretending that we were an old married couple who had said everything there was to say to each other. Would I still be able to just be? I never explained to Dee just what I was doing, but just being next to her, sitting silently made me happy, content.

We were on a common journey, traveling through time and space, learning new things together, sharing experiences that formed lasting memories and shaped the people we were becoming. She brought out the best in me, and I considered myself to be the luckiest man in the world. I was interested in what she was interested in and enjoyed hearing her talk about those things. I found her intellect fascinating. It opened me to things I would not have come to know on my own.

On one level, I wanted to share her with the world. Not that she was mine to share like a possession, but her beauty seemed to shine in the glow of common friends. I was certain everyone else could see that. On another level, I guarded her zealously from others, fearful that someone would steal her from me. I never wanted to lose her.

She had captured me as none before. I wanted my beloved. I loved her playfulness. She could be mischievous, but that made me love her all the more. She would be serious. I loved that part as well. I wanted to be with her all the time. I wanted to do anything and everything for her. I wanted to protect her.

I remember one time Dee was working down the street from her home at a Fotomat. One night when I picked up Dee for a date, she was visibly shaken by something that had happened the night before during her shift. She would never tell me about it. She would just say that it was too painful to even talk about the incident. I was left to imagine the horrors of a robbery attempt, or worse. I wanted to find the perpetrators and beat them up or stand watch in the parking lot during her every shift, but she assured me that her dad and older brother lived closer and could get there within seconds if anything further happened.

I was glad that her brother and father provided this protection, but I wanted to be her protector. In love, it is more important to learn the needs of others than to dwell upon your own. With her, I found it easy to share our ups and downs, our highs and lows.

I remember once, at the end of a date, she paused at her front door and turned back to look at me getting into the car. She just looked at me for a moment, and then she smiled—not the smile she gave to other people, but a smaller one, almost involuntarily, like something she couldn't help. I sat there in the dark after the porch light went off and thought: I would give her anything. I would give her everything I had and everything I hadn't yet become.

CHAPTER 7

Off to College

*Doubt is a pain too lonely to know that faith is
his twin brother.
—Khalil Gibran*

Long-distance relationships are a challenge under the best of
circumstances. I know Dee kept herself extremely busy during her
senior year—perhaps to deflect the loneliness—but I think mostly Dee
enjoyed activity. She never liked to sit still. Her letters arrived full of
news from a life I suddenly wasn't part of: student council votes, softball
games she captained, late nights working on the yearbook. She never
mentioned being lonely, only that she was busy. I pictured her running
from one thing to the next, a blur of activity, and wondered how she
found the energy. Plus, she was a fantastic student, always near the top
of her class.

Going off to college was a mix of thrill and terror. I was on my own
for the first time, navigating class schedules and local bank accounts, a

newfound independence that felt hollow without Dee. The hardest part was simply getting up each day for class, knowing I wouldn't see her.

Talk about having my eyes opened to a whole different world in Ann Arbor. There were National Guard tanks stationed on the perimeter of campus during my freshman orientation. The tanks were there as a precaution in case some kind of trouble broke out, like what was happening on campuses around the country. At the time on other college campuses, there was violence, dissent, disorder, and even a national student strike. Things got so bad that President Nixon established a Presidential Commission to investigate the unrest.

Before I left for college, Dee made me promise to write to her every day. "I want to know everything you are up to at Michigan," she told me. As a parting gift, she made me a ceramic beer stein. It was green, the color of my rival school, not maize or blue, the colors of my school—I think that was Dee being funny—she told me she wanted something for me that would be unique and not something everyone else would have. I treasured its distinctiveness and what it represented.

On occasion, I would use it for its intended purpose. Most of the time, it was a pencil holder. On the face of the mug was an embossing of my name and some decorative features. Inscribed on the bottom simply "to Peaches, with all of my love, Dee." There was a little smiley face above her name and the date, August 1969. I kept it on my desk alongside this fabulous purple egg that she made. The egg was a nod to our first date and the gift that Nicky Arnstein gave to Fanny Brice in the movie Funny Girl. No one ever gave me a marble egg before.

Dee and Sue, the girlfriend of one of my roommates freshman year, combined their artistic efforts on a sailboat wall hanging for our dorm room. Dee found a small piece of driftwood that she used as the hull and then painted a sunset motif on black velvet for the background. She crafted the sails and mast from silver and gold threads wrapped strategically around small nails. The sailboat still hangs in my den.

On top of everything else she had going on in high school, she would come up to see me periodically. The first time Dee came up to campus was just before classes began. We went with one of her high school girlfriends, Cindy, to an off-campus house rented by Cindy's boyfriend. It was a typical campus house, not unlike what you would find near any college—old furniture, small rooms, dimly lit as most renters forgot they needed extra lamps. I didn't know the guy, but I knew Cindy.

The four of us just sat around and talked and listened to music. That was the one necessity in any college house or dorm room: a great stereo with an extensive music library. As the evening wore on, the other couple excused themselves to go into the bedroom.

"You two are welcome to sleep here on the couch," the guy stated matter-of-factly as he walked down the hall to the back of the house. *Welcome to college,* I thought.

I looked at Dee, somewhat in shock. I didn't know what to do next. I had planned on going back to my dorm to sleep that night, but I wasn't comfortable leaving her there alone with another couple in the next room. She kissed me, caressed my cheek, smiled that sweet, innocent smile of hers, and shook her head. We fell asleep in each other's arms on the couch.

Dee was the perfect pen pal. She wrote three or four times a week, or so it seemed. She would write tender letters, funny letters, and even circular letters where I had to turn the paper to read the letter. Dee was supremely confident in herself and in our relationship. She even got a classmate to write to me, a girl I'd jokingly told Dee I had a crush on. It was a silly, ongoing bit between us, and Dee, supremely confident, thought it would be funny to play along.

I always looked forward to walking past the rows of mailboxes in the dorm hall after my morning classes. I'd always feel a small catch in my throat when I saw something in mailbox three twenty-four. More often than not, it was for me and not for either of my two roommates.

I left for college about the same time Woodstock was happening out on Yasgur's farm in New York and beards were de rigueur on liberal campuses across the nation, so I let my hair grow out and grew a beard when I arrived on campus. I thought it was great. It cut down on prep time before class in the morning and kept my face warm in winter. I was fortunate in that after two weeks I had a full growth.

My two roommates couldn't grow a beard to save their lives. I would kid them that they weren't eating enough Jell-O. The keratin in the Jell-O promotes hair and fingernail growth, I would tell them. They started hoarding Jell-O from the dining hall for weeks before giving up.

The problem with the beard was, every time I came home, my mom made me shave it off. I don't recognize you in there, she would tell me. Dee liked it, though—at least I think she did. She always said it tickled, and she loved to run her fingers through it. I loved that part, too.

I had only been at UM for about a month when the phone rang. It was my mom.

"Hi Wally, how are you? How are your classes going? Are you adjusting?"

"Fine, fine and yes." I replied to the stream of questions. Mom was not the type to call and just chat, so I knew something was up.

"I have some bad news. Your grandmother died this morning. I would like you to come home for the funeral."

"Sure, how did she die?" I asked.

"Just old age. She died in her sleep."

"Oh. When do you want to pick me up?"

"Your sister can be there Tuesday about four o'clock. Is that okay?"

I would have to cut some classes for the rest of the week which worried me some that early in the semester but I let my instructors know ahead of time why I would miss class, did a lot of reading at home, and muddled through when I got back.

Carole, my older sister, came and picked me up, and we drove home, mostly in silence. We both had a busy day of classes, and I was trying to mentally plan out how I was going to get my homework done with all the other activities that I knew were ahead of me. The upside was that I would get to see Dee again. Her birthday was that Saturday, and I really wanted to see her.

A couple of days before I got the call from my mom, I had written Dee threatening to come home just to give her a birthday spanking. I wouldn't really do that, just trying to spice things up a bit from my side of the world. The thought of seeing her again overpowered my grief at the loss of my grandmother. She had died a year to the day of our first date.

Dee kindly accompanied me to the wake and the funeral Mass, never leaving my side the entire time. This was not the first family funeral I had attended. My maternal grandfather had passed away when I was ten, and I remember thinking that this was such a strange custom. Having a dead body in a room surrounded by people, most of whom I did not know, staring at my dead grandfather seemed gross to a ten-year-old.

I was glad for the comfort that Dee offered to me, my dad, and my extended family. Somehow, she knew better than I that the true purpose of the wake was to console the living, not to grieve the deceased. And she was quite good at offering comfort. I know my dad appreciated her kind words. I could see it in his eyes, tear-filled as they were.

My paternal grandparents had lived just a block over from us, in a house Grandpa and Dad built together. Grandpa had grown up on a farm in what is now Dearborn, and even after becoming a popular contractor, he never gave up his love of farming. He converted his backyard into an urban farm, and we never bought vegetables all summer. He'd call Mom, tell her to put a pot on to boil, and walk over with a basket of fresh-picked sweet corn. I was glad Dee was with me, a comfort in the face of losing that part of my life.

Dee and I spent as much time together that weekend as we could. After all, it was her birthday weekend. I brought her to dinner at my house on Sunday, a sort of post-birthday celebration. Sunday dinners were always an occasion. With nine of us all dining at once—more if we had company—we needed the dining room table pulled out to its fullest extent.

Dad met Dee at the door that day, and I remember she was wearing a beautiful red coat-dress with dark nylons, as was the fashion.

"May I take your coat?" Dad asked, trying to be helpful to my young friend.

"Mr. K!" Dee exclaimed in sheer embarrassment.

"Walter," my mom admonished, "that is not a coat. That's her dress."

"Well, I didn't know. I am not up on the latest fashion. I apologize, Dee. I hope I didn't embarrass you."

"That's okay. I just didn't expect that comment. Sorry if I offended you with my gasp."

"No, not at all. Come in and sit down. Wally tells me you are a twin?"

"Yes, I have a twin brother."

"Are you identical?" Dad asked, trying to continue the conversation.

"Mr. K!" came another gasp of surprise.

"Oh, I know the plumbing is different. I just wanted to know if you looked alike."

"No, not really. My brother has dark hair and distinct facial features."

"Oh," Dad said, walking off to sit in his favorite chair in the living room, not wanting to risk embarrassing Dee a third time.

Dee was instantly comfortable with the family when she came over for these visits. She fit in quickly, easy and unforced, the kind of girl my mother had probably been picturing for years without knowing it. She and my sisters talked about school and their friends, and we all ate heartily. Mom was a splendid cook. Dee and I helped with the dishes after dinner and then I took her home so that my older sister could drive me back to Ann Arbor before it got too late.

"You have very nice parents, Wally. I think your dad is cute. I liked his comments, even if he embarrassed me more than once."

"Yeah, that was pretty funny. I thought I was the one who was supposed to offer to take off your coat-dress."

"Don't even think about it," Dee admonished with a smile.

I was joking, and she knew it, but she set the boundaries nonetheless.

I wasn't quite ready to take her home, so I drove to Rouge Park and stopped at the top of the toboggan hill in a secluded spot to talk and say our goodbyes.

"Dee," I said, encircling her with my arms. I had my back to the car door, and she was resting with her back pressed against my chest as we talked.

"Yes, dear."

"I've been thinking. How come I don't have a picture of you for my desk at school?"

"I don't know," she said, shrugging her shoulders. "I guess I never thought about it?" She turned her head slightly and kissed me on the cheek.

"Well, Jack and Tom both have photos of their girlfriends, and I would like to have one of you, so I don't forget what you look like."

"You had better not forget me. You'll be sorry."

"I know I would be. I think about you constantly and it would be nice to see your face once in a while when I come home from class, even if it is only in a photograph," I said beseechingly.

"You're right. I'll work on that for you." And she did.

When it was time for me to get home so my parents could drive me back to college, I told her that we had to stop kissing so I could get her home.

"I thought you were going to give me my birthday spanking?" She sounded disappointed.

"Well, I changed my mind. I wanted to be nice to you on your birthday. I don't see you that much anymore now that I am at college."

"Oh!" She giggled.

Dee pressed her face to my chest, when she whispered, "Thank you for making my birthday special." The warmth of her cheek seeped through my shirt and lingered against my heart. I didn't answer at first, only kissed the top of her head, inhaling the scent of her perfume, light and floral, that suited her exactly.

"Oh, you are more than welcome. I thoroughly enjoyed it."

She poked my ribs, half-hearted and grinning.

"We stayed tangled together, talking in the slow, meandering way of people stalling an inevitable goodbye. The afternoon already felt like a memory. I was memorizing the weight of her head on my chest, the smell of her perfume, banking it against the empty weeks ahead. When I finally walked her to the door, her parents' shadows visible behind the curtain, her kiss was quick but firm.

The weeks slid past in a blur of assignments and quiet weekends at the dorm, autumn giving way to bitter cold. I wrote to her nearly every day, long letters about chemistry and my oddball roommates, about the lectures and the food at the dining hall, but mostly about small things that reminded me of her: girls in the cafeteria with hair just like hers, or the song on the radio that made me blush and think of that night at the top of the hill. She replied often, but her notes were dense with doodles and double meanings; every letter a small performance.

Dee was lively, funny, affectionate. She had this way of making ordinary moments feel important.

That Halloween, there was a dance at her high school, and Dee planned out a costume with her friends. She dressed head to toe in a pair of work overalls with aviator goggles and a World War One era cloth aviator helmet on her head. She got Mary Sue to take a photo where she posed, bent over slightly, setting her face in a fierce-looking grimace.

About a month later, there was a note in box three twenty-four, along with a letter from Dee. The note instructed me I had a package and that I could pick it up from the clerk at the counter. I was hoping for some goodies from my mom. I handed the clerk the note, opened the envelope from Dee, and read the letter.

> My dearest Peaches,
>
> Just a quick note to say I am sending you a package today with a photo of me for your dorm room. I hope you like it; it shows my best side. You can hang it over your bed and dream about me each night.
>
> With All of My Love,
>
> dee ☺

"The clerk handed me a tube about two feet long—not the size I expected for a photograph. Back in my room, I quickly unrolled it. It was a poster of Dee."

The playfulness of the poster seemed to motivate me. I threw myself into my studies, my days falling into a rigid routine: class, eat, study, sleep. I wasn't the smartest guy in my dorm; my two roommates had come in with higher grades, but they always seemed to have free time while I was buried in books. They dropped out of engineering after that first year and transferred to the business school. I kept my head down, studying on Saturday nights and learning that the parties where someone 'borrowed' ethanol from the chem lab weren't for me.

Down the road from Michigan was Eastern Michigan University. Eastern became somewhat notorious at the time for its role in the founding of the myth that Paul McCartney was dead. Legend has it that the myth began one Sunday afternoon when a student from Eastern called Russ Gibb, a local radio DJ, and claimed that when you played the Beatle's song "Revolution 9" backwards the voice says, "Turn me on, dead man." Of course, my roommates tried it and later all kinds of other so-called "clues" regarding the alleged death of Paul McCartney were "discovered."

My one indulgence at college was Saturday football. At Michigan, like most college campuses, Football Saturday was an event. Alumni and fans started pouring onto campus for their tailgate parties before most of us crawled out of bed. After stumbling down to breakfast, we would shower and put on our maize and blue. A quick lunch, and it was off for the short half-mile or so walk from campus to the stadium. The closer we got to the stadium, the more students and fans collected around us. It was always packed in the student section. I think they cut the size of the seats in half to accommodate the half-price they charged us for the tickets.

The team got a new coach that year, someone most of us had never heard of, Glenn E. "Bo" Schembechler. The team started slow. They were worse than mediocre the year before, but the fans didn't care, especially the students. We were having too much fun passing coeds up to the top row of the Big House. Most of the coeds didn't mind, but a few objected, thinking it was only an excuse for the engineers to feel a member of the opposite sex. Back then, there were only a few females in engineering, at least at Michigan. There must have been ten males for every female.

The new Athletic Director, Don Canham, broke a long-standing Michigan tradition that year and brought in female cheerleaders. He called them pom - pom girls. This was a thinly veiled attempt to have his freshman daughter on the field.

The team was three and three after the first six games, but suddenly caught fire and began winning consistently. They won the rest of the games leading up to the season finale against hated Ohio State. I say hated because the preceding year, Woody Hayes, the vaunted head coach of Ohio State, after scoring his seventh touchdown, had the gall to go for a two-point conversion. He didn't make it, but still ended with an even fifty points. When asked after the game why he went for two points, Coach Hayes quipped, "because I couldn't go for three." After that, he became hated throughout the entire state of Michigan. I suppose the folks adored him down in Ohio, so it evened out.

Bo had played under Woody and had been an assistant coach at Ohio State. It was the student versus the master. Ohio came into Ann Arbor with sports writers universally proclaiming them the team of the century. Nobody gave Michigan even a ghost of a chance.

As the Michigan team came out of the tunnel that afternoon, they stopped short. Coach Hayes brought his team onto the field first and had marshaled his squad on the Michigan side of the field to warm up. The Michigan team was dumbstruck, but not Bo. He marched right up to Coach Hayes at midfield and said, "Coach you are warming up on the wrong side of the field, you belong down there," he pointed to the other end of the field. Coach Hayes grimaced but marched his team to the other side, where he knew he belonged. He was just playing a little mind game with his old friend, trying to establish his ownership of the entire field. The team and the fans erupted. It was as if we had just won the game. Thus began what was to become the greatest rivalry in college football, the ten years' war.

Michigan went up by a point after the first quarter, and by halftime they were ahead twenty-four to twelve. Both teams went scoreless the rest of the game, and "Meechigan" defeated what many believed was the best college football team ever assembled. It was the only loss that Ohio suffered in two years. The hundred thousand fans in the seats went wild as the final seconds ticked off the clock, pouring out of the stands and swarming the field when it was over. The team carried Bo off on their shoulders, and we climbed on the goalposts and tore them down.

A couple of the guys from our floor were sitting on the crossbar of the goalpost in front of the student section when it came crashing to the ground. The students triumphantly carried the upright from the goalpost out of the tunnel and through the streets of Ann Arbor. One of our floor mates got the idea that this was to become a historic piece of Michigan memorabilia and ran ahead and gathered the rest of us who, by then, had gone to our rooms. We met up with the goalpost on the diag in the middle of campus. Most of the crowd was losing interest by then, so we commandeered the post with our large numbers and brought it to West Quad, Michigan House, where we lived.

We locked it up in a storage closet outside my dorm room and kept it there until we were sure campus police were no longer looking for it. Then we went in and sliced off a one-inch section for everyone in Michigan House. After most of the men on the floor had taken a piece, we needed to trim the remaining section to fit in the trophy case. Since I had the hacksaw and was doing the cutting, I cut a larger five-inch section for myself.

I brought my piece and the rest of the goalpost, about a ten-foot section, to Dee and asked her to paint them so we could memorialize the large section in the third-floor lounge. Being an artist, she accepted the challenge and did a marvelous job, truly worthy of any trophy case on a major college campus. She pasted newspaper clippings on the inside and painted players, the score and headlines on the exterior in blue paint to contrast the original maize already on the post.

We built the trophy case ourselves, placing the goalpost and other memorabilia under glass for all posterity. We were proud of that trophy. Our other major accomplishment as a house that year was getting permission from the University to make Michigan House coed the next year. It was one of the few remaining all-male houses on campus.

But athletics were only a part of college life. The war in Vietnam was never far from our thoughts during that time. Upon reaching the age of eighteen, all males were required to register for the military draft. I had applied for and received a student deferment, meaning I couldn't be drafted until I graduated or left school.

On December 1st, the Selective Service held its first draft lottery, and the campus turned it into a grim holiday. Guys threw parties, as if enough beer could drown out the broadcast. They were drawing birthdays from a glass drum, and the order they came out was the order you'd go to Vietnam. We all crowded into the common room, radios turned up loud, listening for our date of birth and praying it would be one of the last numbers called.

One guy in the room next to us had his birthday selected number seventeen. He was crushed. If he flunked out, he almost certainly would be drafted. He was under a lot of pressure for the rest of the year. They selected my birthday number one hundred seventy-nine. Not bad, I thought, but I wasn't about to give up my deferment. Good thing I didn't. They called up everyone with a draft number of one hundred ninety-five or lower that first year.

The next year, I drew three hundred twenty-five—a safe number. The odds of getting a higher draw before graduation felt slim, so I took a gamble and gave up my student deferment. With my old number, I'd be pushed to the back of the line, safe unless they drafted every single person from the current year first. It felt like a smart move. I never could have guessed that the following year, my birthday would have drawn number three hundred thirty-five.

~

The dorm room phone became a source of dread. The first call told me that my grandmother had passed away. I came home for the funeral, Dee a quiet, steady presence by my side. The second call came in early December, just as the first snow fell. It was my grandfather. Mom always said he died of a broken heart, unable to imagine a world without his beloved wife. After that, I flinched every time a phone rang.

I came home again just before classes ended for the semester. Dee and I spent time together, and we went to see Cactus Flower starring Walter Matthau and Goldie Hawn. I loved Goldie Hawn in her early movies. She reminded me of Dee, not the dumb blonde persona but the looks and the fun-loving attitude towards life.

~

Dee had the grades and test scores for Michigan, no question. She'd worked hard, acing her classes and filling her afternoons with extracurriculars. But we both knew the unspoken obstacle was money. Room and board in Ann Arbor was more than her family could cover, and no amount of dreaming could close that gap.

One evening, she broke the news that she'd been accepted to Wayne State University in downtown Detroit. She'd be a commuter, living at home. She said it with a brave face, but I could see the disappointment in her eyes, and she knew I'd feel it, too.

When Dee told me she'd been accepted to a university thirty-five miles away from me, something in my chest caved in. At Dee's high school, the guys all knew me and my family and, for the most part, respected the relationship Dee and I had. Oh, sure, a few asked her out, but she always refused any one-on-one date. She did go out with large groups of boys and girls and had a great senior year, but was always faithful. I knew that college would be different. There would be no holds barred and the guys would not know me, nor would any of them care.

"What's wrong? I can tell something is bothering you? It will be alright, we can still see each other." Dee comforted me as best she could.

"Dee, college is going to be different. There will be all kinds of guys and you'll be meeting them every day in class, at parties. I just keep thinking about how far away you'll be."

"You're not going to lose me."

"I know that's what we both want. It's just—two more years is a long time."

~

In May of that year, Dee had her senior prom at the Raleigh House in Southfield, and no, I didn't get her any more dandelions. I knew more of the girls than the guys at the prom between Dee's friends and my sister's. I didn't feel like an outsider at all, as sometimes dates do at these things. Many of the young ladies I grew up with and played with when we were children were in attendance. To see these beautiful young ladies dressed to the nines made the evening special.

She took my hand and led me from table to table, then asked if it was okay to dance with some of the guys from her classes. I leaned against a pillar, watching her spin on the dance floor with a boy from her debate team, her laughter carrying over the music. This was her night, a final celebration with the people who had filled her days while I was away. And watching her shine, the center of her own universe, I felt a swell of pride so pure it eclipsed any flicker of jealousy. To love her was to love this, too.

"Thanks for allowing me to be with my friends tonight. I didn't mean to spend so much time with them. I didn't intend to leave you stranded for so long, truly I didn't. Time just got away from me. I just wanted to say goodbye to all my friends."

"Dee, I understand completely and didn't mind one bit. I enjoyed watching you laugh and dance, and have fun. It made me feel good knowing that you had such a great senior year and that my being at college did not dissuade you from having a fabulous time. In many ways, I owe your friends an enormous debt of gratitude for filling in for me and assuring your happiness this past year."

"Oh, Wally ... thank you so much for understanding. I'm so lucky that I found you and picked you up on the bus that day."

"Me too. I think back on that day as the luckiest day of my life."

On the way home that evening, we stopped at Hines Park so that I could begin my scavenger hunt for the garter. I retrieved a pink garter that matched her flowing pink gown. As special as that was, it was even more special spending time with Dee. Now that college was finished for the academic year, I was free to see Dee daily, at least when we were not working.

That summer, I worked at a local City owned golf course. The course itself was fairly challenging, with lots of shots back and forth across the winding Rouge River. I worked concessions, took care of the tee time book or acted as a Ranger, walking the course and reminding the golfers to keep pace with the group in front of them. I also learned to golf that year.

The course pro ran the Free Press golf school for kids during the week, and I learned the basics by assisting him. He never gave me formal lessons, just one piece of advice. "When you're walking the course as a Ranger," he said, "carry a club in one hand and just swing it. It's an old caddy trick to get your hands in the proper position." So, I walked the fairways all summer, swinging a seven iron, letting the rhythm sink into my bones.

Jerry was a scratch golfer back then. He had a drive that looked just like the ones I would see from Jack Nicklaus on TV, starting low and fast, then quickly rising to its peak as the aerodynamics of the ball took over. A well-struck golf shot was a beautiful sight to behold. Jerry knew I was taking up golf that year, and once on my day off, he offered to take me out on the course. Being an employee, I got to play for free, so I had been out once or twice before and felt that at least I would not look like a complete boob in front of him. I had an old set of clubs that I borrowed from one of my uncles who never used them anymore.

Mr. Z was my first and only golf instructor that day. He taught me the proper grip and setup, taught me how to read greens and to hit out of the bunkers. I wasn't that good, averaging two strokes over par per hole for the front nine that afternoon. Mr. Z was one under par.

"Okay, now that you have the hang of the game, how about we make it a little more exciting on the back nine?"

"What do you mean?"

"Let's have a small wager on who will win the last nine holes."

"You have got to be kidding," I laughed. "You'll clobber me."

"No, I have been watching you and I will give you two strokes a hole. That should even things out."

"I don't know," I said cautiously, screwing up the side of my face, thinking I could not afford to lose much money. "What's the bet?"

"If you win, I will buy you dinner. If I win, you have to wash my car."

"Okay, I can afford that. It's a bet," I said, shaking his hand.

I played much better on the back nine and was up by three strokes after the first four holes. I hit a great drive on fourteen and had only a short distance to the green over the Rouge River and down into a valley. Mr. Z had to lay up off the tee box or he would have hit his drive into the river. When I surveyed my next shot, I was thinking I could reach the green with a nine iron or an eight iron. After Mr. Z hit his approach shot onto the green, he came over to me and asked what club I was considering.

"I'm thinking eight iron," I told him, opting for the longer, safer club.

"Oh no, I have been watching your distances and you could never reach the green from here with only an eight iron. You need a seven iron at least. The green is a lot farther away than you think."

I knew that was too much club and that if I hit it correctly, the ball would likely fly over the green and end up out of bounds in the middle of Plymouth Road. But he got me doubting myself and my abilities. I stood there a moment longer than I needed to, running the shot through my head one more time, and somehow the eight-iron ended up back in the bag and the seven was in my hand.

Nice average swing, nice average swing, I kept telling myself. I choked up slightly on the club and made good contact. Just as I expected, the ball flew high over the pin and forty yards past the green, bouncing off the top of the out-of-bounds fence, just barely staying in bounds. Mr. Z was laughing.

"Boy, you caught that one good. You know your distances better than I do."

I just shook my head and slammed the club back into the bag. I learned a valuable golf lesson that day. Trust no one on the course that you have a bet with, even if they are a good friend.

Because my ball was in the rough near the fence and I couldn't take a full swing, it took me seven additional strokes to get the ball into the hole. I was bummed after that catastrophic hole, as I was now down a stroke with four holes to play. I couldn't regain my composure. Mr. Z ended up with a birdie on the last hole and beat me by one stroke.

After we both putted out, I took off my hat and shook his hand on the eighteenth green, congratulating him on the win. He must have felt bad for beating me that way because he bought me dinner anyway. We ate at the Rouge Park Grill, a couple of blocks from the course. We sat and talked man to man, not father of the girlfriend to a young punk kid dating his baby girl. Somewhere between the appetizers and the check, Mr. Z stopped being Dee's father and just became a guy I'd played golf with. Afterwards, true to the bet, I came over the next day and Dee helped me wash his car.

We even had celebrities at the course. Marvin Gaye came through once with his whole entourage. Our manager, who never left the clubhouse, appointed himself Ranger just to watch him play. Hours later, Marvin came storming through the parking lot, cursing and slamming golf balls into the pavement. "Missed a five-footer on eighteen to lose ten grand," the manager told me with a grin. "Walter, go tell him to cut it out before he dents a car."

"Not a chance," I said, putting my head down and returning to my other duties.

The manager just laughed. "Don't blame ya."

We weren't above playing jokes, either. Once, I saw an old hockey teammate hit a tee shot up the blind sixteenth. From my vantage point on the hill, I watched his ball land on the green. When another ranger came to relieve me, I had an idea. I grinned, ran over, and dropped the ball in the hole. We circled back, feigning amazement. "It's in the hole!" The look on my friend's face was priceless. I never did tell him the truth.

~

That same summer, Dee's older brother Gary got married. He chose not to go to college. Instead, her father got him into the electrician's union as a journeyman. He was making good money, found a nice girl, and they fell in love. Near as I could tell, he was the first of my grade school classmates to get married. Dee was in the wedding party, and I was pleased to be invited, even though it meant I had to sit alone for most of the evening.

The bridal party had its own table, and Dee had the obligatory bridal dances to work through after dinner. Then there were the photo sessions, first with the professional photographer, then with all the cameras from the aunts and uncles. Plus, she was such an excellent dancer. Jerry and most of Dee's uncles wanted to dance at least one polka with her. She loved to dance. Mostly I sat at my table and watched. Mr. Z, for reasons I can't explain, came over to me early in the evening and sat next to me.

"What are you drinking tonight?"

"Not much," I shrugged. "I'm driving and I want to be sure to get your daughter home safe tonight."

"It's a wedding. Everyone needs at least one drink." He got up and came back with a stiff glass of whiskey and water and placed it in front of me.

"Now that I have Gary married off, I need to get rid of some of my daughters. Know what I mean?" he said, clapping my shoulder with a wink.

I did, but I just chuckled, not knowing how to respond. Perhaps he wanted a son-in-law to play golf with. Perhaps it was his way of saying I like you, kid, and when you're ready, you have my permission to marry my little girl. Throughout the evening, he kept bringing me more drinks. Eventually Dee figured out just what her dad was up to and stopped dancing with her uncles and came over to dance with me just to get me away from the table of empty glasses. She taught me how to polka that night. The room was spinning faster than she was.

"What was my dad saying to you earlier?" Dee quizzed during my lesson.

"Oh, not much, just that he wants to see you married off. He seemed to be in quite a hurry."

"Stop it, he did not. My daddy loves me," she said, slapping me on the arm.

From every indication I could see, I was certain he did. After we closed the VFW hall down, Mr. Z made sure that Dee drove me home that night. He wasn't taking any chances with his baby girl.

The next morning my head felt like it was being squeezed in a vice, and my mouth tasted like the inside of a coat pocket.

87

CHAPTER 8

The Call

The first kiss is the beginning of that magic vibration that transports lovers from a weightful and measureful world to that of dreams and revelations.
—Khalil Gibran

I moved out of the dorm my sophomore year and into a fraternity. My two roommates from freshman year, to my great surprise, roomed together again in the dorm as sophomores. I say to my surprise because they fought constantly freshman year. They argued over the littlest things and always got under each other's skin. The constant bickering drove me nuts. But in the end, I guess they figured living with the devil they knew was better than living with the devil they didn't.

The fraternity I moved into was a three-story colonial about six blocks east of campus. There were living quarters on the second and third floors, plus three rooms in the basement. On the main floor was a living room, sun room, card room, dining area, and a commercial-grade kitchen. We had a skilled cook at the house, and that was the reason I moved in. I did not want to cook my own meals living in an apartment, and I didn't want to live in a dorm room again and eat quadie burgers.

That first year in the house, I lived in a room in the basement with a senior majoring in Pharmacy, Todge. Nice guy, Polish, never there. He worked weekends in Detroit at Saint John's Hospital to make ends meet, which was fine with me and when he was on campus, he studied at the Med School Library.

What I liked about the room was that it had two built-in desks, two closets, and a private bathroom, complete with a shower. Yeah, it was a lot of work to keep it clean, but it was better than showering in the gross community showers on the second floor. You know how guys keep house.

Todge slept in the room, and I slept in the cold dorm. We had two dedicated sleeping areas on the second floor of the house, each with triple-level bunk beds. In one room, the heat was left on (the warm dorm). There was an adjoining room (the cold dorm) where they kept the heat off and the windows open even through the cold Michigan winters. The cold did not simply fill the room; it claimed it.

The first thing you noticed was your breath. It bloomed in pale clouds above your face, hanging for a moment before dissolving into the darkness. The air carried that unmistakable scent of deep winter—clean, metallic, almost sharp enough to taste.

The cold settled in layers. The tip of your nose went numb first. Then your ears. Fingers tucked beneath the blankets slowly lost their warmth despite rubbing them together. Every exposed inch of skin prickled as if thousands of tiny needles were pressing against it.

The sheets were icy when you climbed into bed, so cold they almost seemed damp, though they were perfectly dry. Yet there was an odd comfort in it, too. Burrowed beneath layers of blankets while snow fell silently outside, you became acutely aware of every small source of warmth—a electric blanket, the knit hat covering your head, the first amber glow of the morning sun creeping across the quilt. In that kind of cold, warmth wasn't something you took for granted. It was something you earned, inch by inch, through the long night.

As the Vietnam War lingered, unrest on campus grew, and there was considerable animosity among the student population towards the draft. The big thing among conscientious objectors was to dodge the draft, even if that meant moving to Canada. The FBI visited the fraternity on one occasion that year. The agents were looking for a brother who had graduated a couple of years earlier.

Some of us were eating lunch at the time and knew as soon as the agents walked into the house that they were likely looking for a draft dodger. Man, did they look out of place on a liberal college campus, strait-laced, close-cropped hair, suits. None of the guys wanted to talk to them or even acknowledge them, so I walked over and volunteered. They identified themselves as FBI and told me who they were looking for. It was a guy I knew as he used to come around the house when I was pledging and we were required to know everyone and a little about each brother. I always thought the guy was a good person. I just couldn't picture him in the military. The agents said he failed to report for duty after being drafted, and they were checking all known addresses of record. I had thought I heard some of the older guys talking the previous year that this guy was planning on crossing the border into Canada until the war was over, so I told the agents what I knew and they thanked me and left.

Life at the house was always, shall we say, different. There was a continuous game going on in the card room. People would join and leave as their classes dictated. On weekends, there were parties or just drinking, at least for some guys. I didn't take part in the drinking or the games that much, never the time or the inclination.

Dee came up early that school year to celebrate her eighteenth birthday on campus. Her father helped her acquire a 1965 polar white Mercury Comet as part of her birthday present, and she wanted to show it off. The car was partly to fulfill a promise her father made to Dee. Because he couldn't afford to send her away to college, he had promised to help her get a car for her birthday. She nicknamed the car the Vomit Comet. It was actually a nice car, and I was always a little jealous since I couldn't afford a car and go away to school. The car Dee wanted was a purple Karman Ghia, a little two plus two sports car. She just didn't have the money for one, even with her dad's help.

It was one of the rare weekends that Todge had some time off from work, and he decided the shower in our room needed painting. Since Dee was available, Todge asked if she would use her artistic talents to help pick out a new color. Not wanting to miss out on a motorcycle ride, Dee jumped at the opportunity. I was left alone, so I just studied until the two of them got back.

When they returned, they were both laughing and giggling like they each had just swallowed a canary.

"Okay, what color did you pick? Not black I hope?" They had threatened before they left to buy black paint, figuring it would hide the dirt so we wouldn't have to clean the shower.

"Oh no, I think you will like this color. It is perfect for this room. It makes a statement," Dee said in her most artistic voice.

I just shook my head, knowing that when Dee started talking like that, it was going to be something unusual, like purple, her favorite color.

She reached into the bag and produced a small can of yellowish-brown paint.

"Brown? Why brown?"

"Oh! This isn't just any brown. It is a very rare shade. They call it 'Baby Shit' brown," she giggled.

"Great! Now I have to shower every day in baby shit."

They both laughed and went about painting the shower together. Good thing I was so understanding.

I loved having Dee come up to visit, and she frequently did. One December weekend, Dee came up and brought her ice skates. She told me ahead of time she wanted to go skating and I was supposed to find a place where we could go. I told her I didn't have my skates at school, but she just said, "So, you can watch me." She did not want to go to a party that weekend. I didn't care. I just wanted to spend time with her.

Down the block from the frat house was Burns Park. Every winter they froze an area as an ice-skating pond for the local kids. We walked to the park that Saturday evening. Dee sat on the bench, took off her boots and put on her skates. I could tell something was bothering her, but she said she wasn't ready to talk about it. I watched her skate for hours. She was so graceful. I didn't mind the cold at all.

Sometimes I would slide back and forth on the ice with my shoes and try to catch her in my arms, but mostly I just watched. When she had enough skating, she changed back into her boots, and we walked back to the frat. We went down to my room to warm up a bit.

After we entered my room in the basement, I locked the door for the night. When I turned around, Dee was unzipping her jeans as if it was the most natural thing in the world. She slipped them off. Underneath she was wearing the cutest little pair of red and blue striped cotton panties, which she left on. She left her top on and climbed into the twin bed. I followed her lead and stripped down to my underwear and climbed into bed next to her. I laid there on top of her, propped up on my elbows, stroking a stray bit of blonde hair that had fallen across her eyes. Those eyes looked at me with that sweet, innocent look that always drove me crazy.

Lying there on top of her, an all-powerful sense of never-ending happiness came over me. I thought, this is where I want to spend the rest of my life, right here between her legs. I wanted to ask her to marry me. But I did not want her to misunderstand my intentions, so instead I asked if she wanted to go to church with me.

There was a midnight Mass on the other side of the campus. It was a long walk, but such a peaceful and fulfilling service. I always felt renewed after Mass was over. Dee was still a little stand-offish after her nap, but at one point during the service while we were standing saying the Our Father, I reached over to where her hand was resting on the pew in front of us and covered her hand with mine. It was as if a jolt of electricity passed between us. But it was not shocking. It was pure happiness. My heart raced and my cheeks felt flushed. I felt a warmth radiating through my body as I felt connected to Dee in a way I never had before. I felt a sense of calm wash over me as I realized how special this moment was and how lucky I was to share it with her. It was as if Dee, and I, and God were the only three people in the universe. I was so grateful to Him for bringing her into my life.

We walked back to the frat hand in hand through the crisp December snow. The metallic crunch of the snow beneath our feet gave an audible indication of just how cold it was. The newly fallen flakes glistened like diamonds illuminated under the streetlights as we passed by. We walked part way in silence.

"Dee?"

"Yes, Wally."

"Are you okay? You seem unusually quiet tonight. Have I done anything to upset you?" I inquired.

"No, not really ... I have just been thinking a lot lately."

"About what?"

"Oh, nothing, just stuff."

"I think about you, too. I miss all the time we used to spend together when I was living at home. It was great when I could just pick up and be at your door in a few minutes."

"Yes, I miss those days, too. It has been so hard on me this past year and a half, as it no doubt has been on you, to have this long-distance relationship."

"I know—I feel so fortunate that we have survived this long through what is a challenging period in our lives. I pray often that we can make it through the next two years."

Dee squeezed my hand a little tighter as we walked through the freshly fallen snow.

The next day, after she left, I found a note she had written the night before. She left it on the side of my desk in a place I would not discover until after she was gone. Just when she had time to write it, I couldn't say.

> Dearest,
>
> Thank you for being so understanding of my moodiness. You are so good to me. I don't know what I would do without you. I want to apologize for the way I treated you this weekend. I had a great many things on my mind and didn't quite know how to put them to words or even if I needed to. Plus, I tend to get moody before my period begins, so that didn't help things. Hope this explains the weekend.
>
> I love you with all my heart,
>
> dee ☺

No explanation was necessary as far as I was concerned, but I appreciated her kind words, nonetheless. That afternoon, I wrote her, thanking her for the weekend and for the note of explanation.

~

My older sister had gotten married the previous month, and every chance she got, she begged me to come visit her and her new husband. I guess she just missed being with her family. After living her whole life in a family of nine, it must have come as quite a shock to suddenly live with only one other person. She and her husband lived in an apartment not too far from Detroit. When I came home for Christmas, I asked Dee if she wanted to go with me on a "double date" with my sister and her new husband.

"Sure, why not."

Carole made us dinner, and afterward she said she wanted to play cards. Not exactly what I was expecting, but she said that she and Jack were a little tired from working and going to school and didn't want to go out anywhere. So, we just talked and played pinochle.

"See, isn't this nice, like two old married couples. Just think, in two years you and Dee will be married and we can do this all the time," Carole said, cheerily smiling at the two of us.

I don't know who was more embarrassed, me or Dee. We both turned bright red.

About ten o'clock, my sister announced it was time for bed, as Jack had to be at work early the next day. I guess that was our signal to leave. We said our goodbyes. I thanked my sister for the lovely dinner, and we walked out into the crisp night air.

"I'm sorry about that," I told Dee as we walked out of the apartment. "I don't know what I was expecting tonight, but it wasn't this."

"No need to apologize. I enjoyed the evening. Anytime I get to spend with you is a wonderful date. It doesn't matter what we do."

That was so true.

It had snowed while we were inside, and we came out to find the old brown Ford station wagon covered in two inches of the white stuff. I opened the passenger car door so Dee could get out of the snow and then went around to the driver's side and started the car. I grabbed the snow brush and set about brushing the car off. There are a lot of windows on a station wagon, so it took a while to clean the car enough so I could drive. By the time I finished, the car was nice and warm, and I was glad for that as I was cold and needed to warm up.

"Ready to go?"

"Yep."

I pulled out of the parking spot and carefully made my way past the rows of apartments, concentrating on the snow beneath the tires, trying to test the pavement to determine just how slippery the roads would be on the ride home.

As we approach the main street, whap. A snowball hit me in the side of the face. I had snow in my ear, on the outside of my glasses, and between my glasses and my face.

Dee just laughed. "You look like a snowman," she giggled.

"Oh, you're in big trouble now, young lady," I said, pulling the car into an open parking spot.

I rolled down my window and grabbed a handful of snow. We had a snowball fight right inside the car. It didn't last long. Dee squealed at the cold of the snow, saying, "I give up. I give up."

Dee tenderly kissed me on the cheek, and smiled. We rolled up the windows and caressed each other, preferring to kiss and watch the snow fall. It was so beautiful. It seemed to twinkle in the glow of the streetlights as we watched. Winter snow can be just so romantic. I cleaned the snow off my glasses as we sat watching the snow fall.

~

"Like Dee, each snowflake is unique." I learned that in high school. One of my classmates did a science experiment one year on factors affecting snowflake formation. He had worked out a deal with the faculty that if it snowed during class, he would be excused so he could go out and collect samples. He would run around trying to catch a single flake on a microscope slide, then he would instantly seal it in acrylic to preserve its shape before it melted. That first snow, after collecting a few samples, Sam came back into class dejected.

"No snow," he exclaimed.

Huh? We could see the white stuff falling. This couldn't just be cotton from heaven.

He informed us it was actually a soft frozen rain and that the atmospherics were such that the flake would not form. He dubbed it, "no snow" to distinguish it from "snow."

As for the embarrassment of my sister's comment, by then we were used to hearing similar comments from within our circle of friends. When the girls would get to talking about plans after college, they generally dismissed us first. "Oh, Dee and Wally are getting married right after college," they would always say. We got used to hearing it. It was just when my sister saw that same emotional bond between us and said it out loud that it came as quite a shock. There was this special glow we exuded whenever we were together, and I guess it was evident to everyone.

~

Dee came up again early the next year to visit me on campus. I was the social chairman of the frat that year and had planned a party for Friday. I always felt a little awkward about this as most of the parties were on Friday and Dee usually couldn't make them as she had classes late in the day and I was never interested in going to the parties alone or finding a date on campus. This time, she said she was coming up for the entire weekend. She wanted to spend some time with her high school girlfriends at Eastern Michigan University and some time with me. In my mind, that meant she was coming to the party, as I was sure I had told her about it.

I was looking forward to this party. By nine o'clock, Dee wasn't there, and I was getting worried. Had something happened to her? Was she in an accident? I sat in my room anxiously waiting to see her walk through the door, or at least hear from her by phone. The music was blasting overhead. When she finally called, she said that she had stopped by Eastern on her way up and was having such a good time that she wanted to stay with the girls. I must have sounded very disappointed. I told her okay and that I would see her the next day, then hung up the phone. I started crying. I didn't want to be in the house anymore, so I went for a walk around the block and when I came back, I sat on the front porch for a while.

One of my fraternity brothers came out looking for me. "Hey there's some girl that's been calling on your room phone and the house phone for the past hour. Guess she really wants to talk with you."

I walked inside and picked up the house phone. "Hello," I said with a finger in the ear away from the phone to block out some of the noise from the party.

"Wally, is that you? I can hardly hear you."

"Yes, it's me. Sorry for all the noise. The party is going full swing. Can I call you back from my room so I can hear better?"

"Sure," she said, giving me the number I could reach her at.

I trudged to the basement and called Dee.

"Hi."

"I have been worried about you ever since you hung up the phone. You didn't sound right. Is something wrong?"

"No, not really. I was just so looking forward to seeing you tonight that when you told me you were staying in Ypsi, I guess I was a little down and you probably picked up on that in my voice. I so wanted you to see the house decorated for the party before it was destroyed," I said, my voice still sounding weak and forlorn.

"I can come over now and see you, would that be okay?" Dee said, trying to cheer me up.

"I guess. But the party will be winding down by the time you get here. So, it's okay if you wait until tomorrow."

"No, I think not. You still sound down. I'll be there in an hour. I just want to finish a few things with the girls here."

"Okay, thanks. I don't know what I ever did to deserve you."

My spirits rose at the prospect of seeing Dee again. When she arrived, it was late, but I didn't care. I was waiting for her on the front porch. When I saw her drive up and park her car in front of the house, I walked over and gave her a big hug and a kiss to thank her for coming.

"I want to apologize for my sulking tonight. I guess it is just my turn to be moody. I had such a tough week and so wanted to see your face. I have been thinking about you more than usual this week, counting the seconds until the weekend. It's just when you said you wanted to spend time with your girlfriends, it kinda burst my bubble a bit and I wasn't prepared for it. I appreciate your understanding and taking the time to visit. I know it's difficult for you to always be the one doing the driving but I just can't afford a car at this point in my life what with all the other expenses at school," I said as we walked side by side holding hands as we moved towards the front door.

"Oh, Wally, you don't need to apologize to me. I love you and was looking forward to seeing you too. I didn't mean to hurt your feelings, truly, I didn't."

"I know you would never hurt me on purpose. I can't imagine you hurting a fly, let alone another person. I am so lucky to have you as a friend ... my best friend ... my love..."

I squeezed her hand, and we walked into the house. Most of my fraternity brothers had gone to bed already, or were out taking their dates home, or wherever. We walked down the stairs to my room. Dee sat on the chair, and I sat on the bed. There wasn't a lot of furniture in the small room, and I didn't want to sit in my desk chair. The position on the bed was closer to her, and I wanted to be as close to her as possible.

Physical contact was always slow in coming as our time apart increased. Anyone who has had a long-distance relationship knows there must be a readjustment period. Dee had on one previous occasion made it clear that she did not want to be simply a sex object. I never consciously treated her as one, but she must have worried about it from time to time. Not that she wasn't physically attractive, she was. But I understood. It was just so hard after not seeing her to hold off on racing over to just hug her to death and kiss her until my lips were chapped.

I understood her need for time to readjust, to talk, and to rekindle what we had and I tried to curtail this burning desire to skip this part and race to the kiss. I knew we had such precious little time together at those meetings that I couldn't bear to waste a single second. After particularly hard weeks, the anguish of waiting grew almost unbearable.

As Dee sat in the chair, I could see she was dozing off. She must have had such a long day, and the emotional stress of having to deal with a moody boyfriend put her over the edge. I talked about my week and my classes, and how I missed her. In the end, I became content to simply watch her sleep in the chair. God, she was beautiful! My angel, my all. I couldn't help but smile. I wanted so much to sit on the edge of her chair and stroke her hair, caress her cheek, make tiny circles on her arm with my finger, just to touch her would be heaven. I resisted, not wanting to wake her. She needed her rest. For now, I was content just to be in the same room with her.

Eventually, sleep overcame me. I dreamed the dreams of a man deep in love, knowing his beloved was close at hand, close enough that he could touch her.

The next day, we had breakfast and enjoyed our time together. We walked around campus. I repeated many of the things I had spoken to her the night before when she was asleep in the chair. We laughed at the silly birds darting in and out of the ivy covering the buildings and lovers holding hands. We were holding hands too, but that was different. It was so natural to hold onto her slender hand. It was as if her hand was an extension of my own and not something belonging to another person.

I was instantly transformed at the slightest touch from her, brought back to our earlier time together when we laughed often and loved completely. Not that we were physically intimate together; this was never the case. I was not ready for that major step in my life, and I was pretty sure Dee was not either. Because of our shared religious beliefs, we grew up knowing this level of love was reserved for married couples.

And we kept our faith intact. But it was difficult. After all, this was the Age of Aquarius, Hair, Woodstock, and free love.

We went traying in the Arb that afternoon. Traying was the college equivalent of sledding. You would borrow a dinner tray from the cafeteria and use it as a sled. We could lock our legs around the person in front of us to form a makeshift toboggan. Those were particularly difficult to control going down the hills, as you had to rely on everyone maintaining their balance and all leaning in the same direction at the same time. One false move and the entire chain would topple.

Traying was a favorite winter pastime on campus. The arboretum was on the northeastern edge of campus. A secluded area with evergreen trees lining the rolling hills. At the far northern end of the Arb was the Huron River, a lazy meandering stream wide enough and deep enough for canoes and kayaks that were always in evidence when the river was not frozen. A walk through the winding paths of the Arb was always peaceful, except during traying season.

We went to Saint Mary's midnight Mass that evening, and if anyone was ever offered a glimpse of heaven, I was afforded the distinct pleasure every time I attended Mass with her by my side ... at once at peace, but so much more. Filled with an overpowering sensation that is impossible to put into mere words. When you experience it, you want to stay in that altered state for all eternity. And I so wanted to stay right there forever.

The congregation at midnight Mass was mostly students and some faculty members. I had been in a lot of churches in my brief life up until then. In most, there were lots of distractions. Kids crying, young adults there only because their parents were forcing them to go, people coming late and leaving early. Here it was different. Nobody was being forced to attend. We were all there because we wanted to be. That brought an inner peace that seemed to overtake the entire congregation. To be sure, the times I was there with Dee were enhanced by several orders of magnitude. Pure heaven. I could actually feel God's touch.

We walked home hand in hand after Mass. Dee spent the night in my basement room, and I slept in the cold dorm. I was at the pinnacle of happiness. The next day, Dee took her shower in the baby-shit brown enclosure she helped paint earlier in the school year.

"Gawd, that's a horrid color. How could you let me do that to you? I could not stand showering in there every morning," she complained as she dried her hair with a towel.

"I think of you every time I shower and the color fades into a brilliant shade of love. I don't mind at all," I told her, smiling at the thought that she had finally come to realize the absurdity of her original color choice.

"Oh, you are just too silly." She kissed me, and I smiled.

We shared breakfast, and Dee had to leave. She wanted to see her girlfriends at Eastern one more time before heading back home. I kissed Dee goodbye and watched her drive off in that white Mercury Comet until it disappeared down the road and over a hill. I missed her already.

I walked back to my room and began studying. I was the house KOLB (keeper of liquor bills) at the fraternity. It was a position that fell to whoever occupied the room next to the noke machine. The noke machine was a Coke machine with a twist. We kept Coke in two columns and put beer in the other three. Because beer was more expensive, we would put a beer in every other slot, so you had to put in twice the amount of money to get the beer. I kept the machine filled and did the ordering and banking. I also provided change for the brothers when they needed it.

I was lapsing into a melancholy when Jim, one of the fraternity brothers, came in asking for change. He didn't need change. It was just an excuse to start a conversation. I knew he was not a coke drinker, and he didn't drink beer except at parties. Word had gotten around that I had a female in the room the previous night and he wanted details. He was a bit of a jerk, and I was not about to give him the satisfaction.

"So, how was your friend? Is she gone now?"

I didn't answer, just continued counting out his change.

"Hmm. You know, you are not being fair to her. Any girl who spends the night in this house automatically gets labeled. Is that really what you want to do to her?" he began lecturing me.

Now I was getting mad. *What a hypocrite*, I thought. I knew Jim had at least two different girls spend the night in his room since I had moved into the house. But he kept pursuing this line of questioning, trying to see if I would provide details of the previous night as if a bet with some of the other brothers held in the balance.

"You need to consider her feelings and what other people think of her and her reputation."

I thought *I had better hand him his change before I punch him in the nose*.

"Here's your change. Now get out of here. I have to study," I said more angrily than I should have.

"Oh, okay." He shrugged his shoulders and left, recognizing that I would not tell him what he came to find out.

At that point, I was furious. That peaceful place where I existed only a few hours before was shattered, and I could not bring it back. He had gotten to me, and I could not get his words out of my head. They kept rolling around in my brain. *Was I being unfair?* I didn't mean to be, but maybe I was. *Should I worry about what other people think, even if I don't respect their opinions? Was I hurting my precious?* Too many thoughts rushing too quickly.

When I wasn't studying, I began focusing on the issue. Should I make an "honest" woman of her in the eyes of others, even though we did nothing to be ashamed of? I probably should not have her stay in the room anymore, even if she slept in the bed and I slept in the cold dorm.

How would I support her if we got married?

Did I love her enough to marry her?

Should I leave Michigan to be with her at Wayne?

The more I thought about it, the more depressed I got. It was driving me mad. How could I support Dee in the manner that I would want at this point in my life? I could barely cover my college expenses, let alone support another person.

I didn't have the courage to quit Michigan knowing that in the long run it would be better for my career and equip me to be a better provider. My depression and questioning spilled out into my letters.

Instead of signing them "with all my love," I began using "love" then it turned to "peace." I was the one seeking inner peace in my thoughts and I did not stop to consider how my love would interpret the change, a serious error in judgment on my part. Dee immediately noticed the change and asked me about it. The change, no doubt, worried her greatly.

~

Spring was a wonderful time on campus. It was tradition at the fraternity that when the temperature reached sixty-nine degrees for the first time each year as measured by the sign on the bank at the corner of South University and East University everyone was to cut classes, go back to the frat, sit on the roof of the house and drink beer. As the KOLB it was my job to make sure there were sufficient supplies on hand for the occasion.

Spring break also afforded me some much-needed time away from school and a chance to go home and spend some time with my girl. Dee wanted me to go with her to sit in on some of her classes at Wayne while I was on my spring break. Her break did not coincide with mine, so I happily agreed. Any chance to spend time with her was time well spent.

Dee drove us down to campus where I bumped into my brother-in-law as we were parking her car and he invited me to attend one of his senior level engineering classes just so I could compare them with the ones I had at UM. I was more interested in being with Dee but he insisted, wanting I think to show me just how difficult classes were at Wayne and so we compared schedules. Jack had only one class that day: thermodynamics. Dee had two, one of which overlapped the thermo class. I asked Dee if it would be okay if I sat in on one class with each of them, and she agreed.

Wayne and Michigan have different educational philosophies. At Wayne, they emphasized the practical. At UM, they emphasized the theoretical. Neither is better, just different. When I attended the senior-level class, my basic foundation in the theoretical side of thermo allowed me to understand the practical skills being taught even without reading the material. It just made sense to me as a logical extension of what I already knew.

After I had attended the thermo class, I found out that Dee was having a test in her biology class and there would be no lecture or lab that day. She wanted me to attend the other class she had, but I didn't know until it was too late. I just sat through the exam and watched her. Her instructor thought it odd to have an outsider sit through an exam, and she monitored me throughout the period just to ensure I wasn't slipping Dee any answers.

When Dee had finished answering all the exam questions, she took me to the cafeteria for lunch, and we sat and ate. A couple of guys came by to say hello and chat briefly with her, and at least one of them had to be in her bio class because they were comparing notes and discussing the test.

"Hey, Dee."

"Oh, hi Mike. What did you think of the test?"

"Not as bad as it could have been. What did you put down for the question on the discovery of microorganism?"

"Leeuwenhoek"

"Man, I missed that one. I couldn't pull the name out of my memory bank. Well, I'll see ya later. I have to get to my lab."

"Who were those guys" I asked after they left.

"Oh, just friends," she replied quietly. "The one you just met is Mike."

On spring break, we walked for hours talking about these things and what I was thinking about. I explained some details, but not all of them. I told Dee I was trying to decide if we had a future together and if we should get married. This shocked her, and she cried. I cried too. I was phrasing this all wrong, and I knew it, but I did not know how to say exactly what was in my heart. I wanted to be with her desperately, but what I truly wanted was for her to be happy. More than anything, she deserved to be happy. I did not like seeing her cry.

"Dee, do you think we have a future together?" I asked somewhat abruptly.

"Why would you even ask that?" Dee cried.

"I don't know, it's just that I have been thinking a lot about this kind of stuff lately and seeing you with those other guys today brought these thoughts to the forefront," I said shrugging my shoulders.

"I'm not ready to get married. It's not what I want from you at this point in my life, Wally. I want to finish college. But I need to know that you still love me."

"Oh, Dee, I love you with every fiber of my being. I'm just thinking about what is best for you. I worry I am being unfair in asking you to maintain this long-distance relationship. At this point in my life, I fear you need more than I can give you.

"Just you worry about yourself. I will decide what is best for me," she said sternly.

"I didn't mean it that way. Believe me, I understand all too well that I can't decide your fate. Your destiny is your own. I can only hope that in some small way I can be a part of it." I tried to be apologetic, but woefully missed the mark. We cried some more. We must have cried and talked for hours. I don't think that either of us ate that afternoon or evening. Nourishment of the body was far from our thoughts. We were seeking nourishment for the soul. We reached her porch and sat down from our long, circuitous journey.

"I could never love another. If, for whatever reason, you find another man, I will take it as a sign that God wants me to reconsider my secular lifestyle and I will give serious thought to becoming a Catholic priest," I confided, looking deep into her eyes.

"Oh, Wally, I know you would make a wonderful priest, but I think in your heart you know you will always need to be loved."

She was right, of course, but I still made a mental promise to myself.

As many young Catholic boys no doubt did, I played at saying Mass in my basement when I was in grade school. I built myself a small tabernacle out of scrap wood and my mom stitched together a veil out of powder blue material she had lying around her sewing area for me to cover the makeshift tabernacle. I used a small cup that fit inside the opening I made as the chalice. But that was in the past. When I discovered girls, I lost much of my interest in the priesthood.

Spring break concluded with me believing we were in a good place. We had come to an understanding about the things I needed to do. Dee expressed her deep concern with the closing I was using in my letters.

"Were you trying to give me the brush-off, to tell me you had grown tired of me, that you no longer loved me?" Dee asked.

"I apologize, Dee. I don't know what possessed me to change. I was not trying to give you the brush-off by any means. My feelings towards you haven't changed. After this weekend, I can honestly say that my belief that we have a future together is as strong as ever. In the past, I never even gave this a thought ... I just knew we would always be together. Now, in part because of the prolonged distance gap, I admit from time to time I have doubts. I know you have many good friends at Wayne and it would shock me if at least some of them weren't male, as I saw this past week. I worry that at some point I will lose you to distance, a better man, or both."

"Oh, Wally, let's try to not let that happen."

And we tried. I called more often and wrote to her more often, and I hoped that this difficult period was now in the past.

Dee began listening to the poetry of Rod McKuen and let me borrow her copy of one of his albums, "The Sea."

It spoke to me.

> I'd like to crawl behind your eyes
> and see me the way you do
> or climb through your mouth
> and sit on every word that comes up through your
> throat.
> Maybe I could be sure then
> maybe I could know
> as it is—I hide beneath your frowns
> or worry when you laugh too loud.
> Always sure a storm is rising.
>
>
> Perhaps the time will come
> when I no longer smile the way I did this morning
> or last week.
> When you no longer turn just so in bed
> or on the street.
> People drift apart as they come together
> only the going away is slower
> If it comes that time of leaving
> Maybe the sea will say of us
> They loved one Sunday

> The tide came in and the tide went out
> I do love you—believe that
> And if I've ever been unfaithful
> It's only with my friend, the sea.

The words expressed what was in my heart, and I took solace in listening to the album over and over. It always made me think of her.

Then came "the call".

"Wally?"

"Hi, Dee. I am so glad to hear your voice. I was going to call you later this week. I have an exam tomorrow that I have been studying for, but I needed to talk with you again."

"Oh, well, I won't take away too much of your study time. I just needed to tell you something. A guy I met at Wayne asked me out on a date. I want to say yes, but I wanted to tell you in advance. I didn't want you hearing about it from anyone else but me."

"Well, I appreciate that. I can't say I'm surprised. I have been expecting this call ever since you told me you were going to Wayne and not Michigan. I don't know what else to say. I want you to be happy, but honestly, I hoped I was the one who would make you happy. Is there still a chance for me?" I asked, almost begging for a positive response.

"Oh, Wally, how can you ask that? I still love you. I want you to know that. But I want to see how things go with this guy. His name is Mike, and he seems very nice."

"Well, I'm sure he is. At least I know he has excellent taste in women. Please let me know how things go and I will try not to worry too much," I said as bravely as I could muster.

"Okay, it's a deal. I promise I will keep you posted. And please try not to worry."

~

A few weeks later, there was a second call.

"Wally?"

"Hey, Dee, great to hear your voice. You sound happy."

"I am."

"So, what's new?"

"Not much. I just wanted to see if you were coming home this weekend. I really need to see your face."

"I hadn't planned on it. With final exams coming up, I am behind and I am worried about not having enough time to review all the material I need to."

"Oh!" The disappointment in her voice was palpable.

"Can you change your mind? I really, really need to see you." Her tone was one of supplication.

"I'd rather not."

"Oh ... how come every time you need to see me I drop everything I'm doing and drive up to see you, but you can't come down to see me just once?"

"Dee? How can you say that? I come home a lot."

"Well, not enough." Her voice sharpened.

"I know. You have told me I need to work harder on that part of our relationship. It is just so hard to get back and forth without a car." I knew excuses would not cut it at that point, but I started making them, anyway.

"Well, maybe I'm not worth the extra effort."

Panic set in. I didn't like the direction this conversation was heading and needed to change its course. Dee clearly wanted to tell me something but didn't want to do it over the phone. I knew in my heart what was coming, and I began to cry.

"Oh, Dee. You are more precious to me than gold," I choked out through my tears. The words from the Book of Wisdom raced through my head.

> I preferred her to scepter and throne, and deemed riches nothing in comparison with her, nor did I liken any priceless gem to her; because all gold, in view of her, is a little sand, and before her, silver is to be accounted mire. Beyond health and comeliness I loved her, and I chose to have her rather than the light, because the splendor of her never yields to sleep.
>
> Yet all good things together came to me in her company, and countless riches at her hands.

"Well, you certainly don't show it." Her tone was defiant.

Tears filled my eyes.

"Okay Dee, I'm on my way," I choked out through my tears. "I will be there as soon as I can figure out how to get home." I hung up the phone. I couldn't help but think back to the call from a few weeks earlier. I shook my head, remembering the hurt I felt. I recalled every word, every inflection in her voice.

"Todge, can I borrow your car?"

"You know the rules. You can't ask me. I told you at the beginning of the year when you moved in that my insurance does not permit me to let anyone else drive the car."

"Yeah, I know, but this is an emergency."

"Why, what happened?"

"Well, you heard the conversation with Dee just now?"

"Yes."

"Then you know I need to see her right away."

"Relationship problems are not emergencies. Find another way home," he grumbled, and went back to studying.

I called another friend who had a car. No luck.

I put on my shoes, grabbed my coat, and ran out of the fraternity.

I hitchhiked down Washtenaw toward home. I got a ride from someone heading past Ypsi but not going all the way to Detroit. The driver let me off on Michigan Avenue, and I began thumbing for a ride again. There was scant traffic at that time of night, so I began running. I ran for about five miles, turning to stick out my thumb every time I heard a car approach. No luck.

I was out in the country between two cities and there were no phones. This was before the era of cell phones and I found myself stuck, too far from Ann Arbor to turn back, too far from home to make it walking before about one in the morning. I was in no-man's-land, both physically and emotionally.

I kept running until I reached a gas station that had a phone. I called Todge and begged him to come get me. By the grace of God, he relented and picked me up.

"You're an idiot for even trying to hitchhike at this hour."

He was right, of course, and I didn't care. I just knew that I had to get home. I hardly spoke a word the entire rest of the way into Detroit. Todge dropped me off at the corner of Southfield Freeway and Joy Road, about a mile from Dee's house.

"Can you at least make it from here?" he said, still mad at me for interrupting his studies.

"Yes, thank you so much. I really owe you for this."

Todge sped off, squealing his tires, hoping to get back to his books, as he had a pharmacological exam coming up and needed to study.

I raced the rest of the way. Each stride brought me closer to the one I loved, closer to the answer to that lingering question. I began walking once I reached her house, dreading what might lie ahead, pausing to catch my breath. One by one, I climbed the stairs. I was standing now on that fateful spot where we shared our first kiss. My knuckles tapped lightly on the aluminum frame before me.

Dee answered the door and was surprised to see me so late in the evening. Tears lingered in her eyes, eyes that even then captured me.

"I didn't think you were coming."

"I knew I had to. I knew from the tone in your voice that this was more than just a casual request on your part. Sorry it took so long. Is it okay to talk now?"

"Maybe we can sit on the porch for a while." Dee didn't want an audience for this conversation.

I nodded, the thinnest of smiles my visible shield. I desperately wanted to kiss her lips, but her face told me now was not the time.

"So, can you tell me what's bothering you?"

"I don't know," she started, afraid to continue.

"Please try."

"Wally, I think I'm falling in love."

In my heart, I knew this was what was coming. I just didn't want to hear the words fall from her mouth.

"I see," I choked out.

"I didn't mean for it to happen. It just kinda snuck up on me."

"I see," I said, shaking my head. I bit my lower lip, trying to hold back the tears.

"Are you mad?"

"No. How could I ever be mad at you? Disappointed? Yes. Worried? Yes. Sad? Definitely."

I held her hand and let her talk. I didn't hear much of what she was saying. All I could think about was the emptiness that would be my life without her. It was not a prospect that I relished. It wasn't long before her dad poked his head out the door. "Dee, time to say good night," he whispered.

"Okay, Dad, I'll be in shortly."

"Wally, I need to go in now. Can I see you tomorrow?"

"Sure." I kissed her goodbye. This time, though, the kiss was different. Something was missing. I couldn't put my finger on it at the time, but I worried about it all the way home.

I ran back to my house and I think I shocked my family when I walked in the door so late at night without so much as a hint that I was coming home. I made some lame excuse then said I was tired and wanted to go to sleep and would talk more in the morning. Good thing it was night. I was hoping Mom couldn't see the tear stains on my cheeks. I walked downstairs to the room I shared with my two brothers.

The next day I got up, showered, sat down for a hearty breakfast and updated my family about school, exams that were coming up, everything but the real reason I was home.

"Are you planning on seeing Dee while you are home?" Mom asked, knowing I always split my time at home between the two houses.

"I guess," I said, looking down at my plate, knowing full well that I was going over there that afternoon.

After lunch, I asked to borrow the family station wagon, and I drove over to Dee's house.

The first question I asked Dee was, "Do I still have a chance or is it over?"

"Oh, Wally, we have been through too much together to give up so easily. Yes, I think we can work through this. It will be hard and there will be lots of tears, but if it is to be, it will be. I do so want to try."

Relief! I don't know what I expected that afternoon, but just hearing her say I was still in the game was an enormous weight off my shoulders.

"Okay, where do we go from here?" I knew I was not calling any of the shots. Things were completely in her control and out of mine.

"I'm not sure. Let's just take it slow ... day-by-day. Would that be okay?"

"More than okay." A wave of relief swept over me at the thought that things were not ending. "Would you mind if we go for a walk?"

"I'd like that."

I reached for her hand, not actually touching it but holding my hand out, almost pleading for her to place her hand in mine. She finished the simple gesture, and we walked hand in hand for miles. I cherished each additional step we took together, each additional word she spoke, knowing each one might be the last. There were tears from both of us and there were smiles as we reminisced about the times we shared. We were building back the relationship, I thought, and I was so grateful. I had lost her and now saw a ray of hope. In retrospect, I can see now that Dee was seeking closure on our time together.

"What about Mike?" I asked about her new interest.

"I don't know. I do like him, but my heart still belongs to you. I can't truly love another man while my heart is not my own." She was pleading for me to release her, but I was blind to this supplication.

Relief! I thought. "Why does love have to be so difficult? Isn't it supposed to be the easiest thing in the world?"

"Love is the easiest thing in the world and the most difficult at the same time. It comes naturally, yet requires constant effort."

I nodded.

"Thank you for coming home this weekend. I really needed to see you and talk to you."

"I know. And I needed to see your face again. To see that little twinkle in your eye. Yes, there it is."

"Oh, stop it, you're just embarrassing me now," she said, slapping me on the shoulder.

"Sorry, I just can't help myself sometimes." I was glad to see her smiling again. It gave me a warm feeling inside. When I went back to school, I felt confident that we were on the right track toward building a stronger relationship than we had in the past. In one of her letters that followed, Dee suggested I read one of her favorite poets, Kahlil Gibran, on love. Clearly, she had been thinking deeply about all these things.

When love beckons to you, follow him,

Though his ways are hard and steep.
And when his wings enfold, you yield to him,
Though the sword hidden among his pinions,
may wound you.
And when he speaks to you, believe in him,
Though his voice may shatter your dreams,
as the north wind lays waste the garden.
For even as love crowns you, so shall he crucify you.
Even as he is for your growth, so is he for your pruning.
Even as he ascends to your height and
caresses your tenderest branches that quiver in the sun,
So shall he descend to your roots
and shake them in their clinging to the earth.

CHAPTER 9

Good Friday

*Let there be no purpose in friendship save the
deepening of the spirit.*
—Khalil Gibran

Classes ended April 9th, Good Friday, the start of Easter break. It was a warm, sunny day, mid-sixties. My sister Carole picked me up and brought me home. As was my usual pattern, I spent some time with my family when I first came home. About seven o'clock, I called Dee to make arrangements to see her on Saturday.

"Hey, Dee. How are things?"

"Okay, when are you coming over?"

"Oh, I am a little tired tonight. I thought I would spend the evening at home with the folks. Can I see you tomorrow?"

"No," came the curt reply. "I have a date with Michael."

I had completely forgotten I was sharing her with another man.

"Okay, can I see you now?"

"Yes. I think that would be best. I have some things to say to you and I want to do it face to face."

Oh, man, this is it, I thought.

"Okay, Dee, I'll be right over," I whispered.

I grabbed the keys to the station wagon and made the short trip though not with my usual joy in seeing her again.

"Where'd you want to go?"

"I don't care, anyplace."

We sat in the car in front of her house and talked. I did not want to be driving during this conversation.

"You said on the phone that you have some things you want to say?"

"Yes." Dee didn't seem to know where to start or if she even wanted this conversation.

"Well?" I didn't want to proceed with this conversation either, but I knew in my heart that it was inevitable.

"Wally, I know you have tried very hard these past few months. You have put forth so much effort to build back what we once had, but it was too little too late."

Here it comes, I thought, shaking my head. I turned my face from hers, looking out the front windshield of the car, not wanting her to see the tears that were welling in my eyes. I pursed my lips, trying desperately to hold back the sobs that I could tell were building up within me.

"I have fallen in love with this other guy and I can't go on bouncing back and forth between the two of you. I'm tired of it. It's too hard on me. I have given this a lot of thought and have made my decision."

"Oh, Dee," I started.

"Stop, I don't want to hear it. I've spent too many nights already crying over you. I refuse to spend any more. I don't love you anymore and I need to be free of you, to get you out of my life. I can't keep seeing you. It's just too difficult."

Dee stated her feelings far more emphatically than I could have anticipated. The sharpness of the blow from those words stung me like no other. Better she stab me with a knife in the heart. It would have hurt less and healed faster.

I searched her eyes for a glimmer of hope. There was none. What I saw frightened me to the depths of my soul. *How could I have hurt this beautiful individual so deeply that she would say these things? What did I do wrong? This can't be.*

She vented her anger, and I sat there in silence and took it. Her words were cruel, but I told myself she was just hurt. I deserved them anyway. Still, they landed like punches, each one deeper than the last, but I sat there in silence. I knew she didn't really hate me; she was upset, struggling, and I tried to understand. I had never seen her so upset, so angry, and I began to worry about her. Whether there was something deeper.

I felt spent when the avalanche of rage was over, even though I just sat there and took it all, like a beating. I sat in silence, knowing there was nothing I could say that would change her mind. I still loved her. In my heart, I knew I would always love her. I just didn't want to accept the fact that she no longer loved me.

When she had said all that she wanted to say to me that evening, I walked her quietly to her door. I leaned in to kiss her goodnight as I always did at the end of our time together, but she placed her hand on my chest to stop me and pulled her face away from mine. She would not let me kiss her.

My lips grew sad knowing that they would never again taste the sweetness of her kiss. Gone was my radiant moon; the dark that was the night poured over me. I drove home in unfathomable sorrow, with my hands loose on the wheel, the road ahead meaning nothing, arriving somewhere I hadn't chosen. The seat beside me held only air. I had lost a piece of my soul.

~

Melancholy gripped me throughout the night. When I woke up the next day, I needed to do something, anything; anything that would bring me closer to her. After lunch, I visited the florist on the corner of the street where she lived. I picked up a dozen white daffodils, like the first flowers I ever bought her. White for fidelity, humility, beauty—things I thought we had. Daffodils for a new beginning, though not the one I had ever wanted. A beginning for Dee and Mike. A beginning for me too, but one without her. As I traced my fingers over the delicate petals, I wondered if she'd even notice them. If she'd know they were from me. If she'd understand what I was trying to say in the only way I knew how.

I walked out the front door of the florist shop, flowers in hand, and I looked down the street. I saw her house across Joy Road. Four houses from where I stood. The house I visited on so many occasions. The one that held so many memories. How I longed to knock on that door or just sit on the porch, hoping she would come outside and talk. Turning, I walked in the opposite direction. Tears filled my eyes.

That evening, after I was certain Mike had picked her up, I lingered on the corner, staring at the house that once felt like a second home. The lights cast long shadows on the porch where we'd kissed goodnight so many times. My grip on the bouquet tightened. For a moment I thought about turning back, pretending for one more night. But it was no use. It was over.

I walked up to the porch and stood on the very spot where Dee and I shared our first kiss. I placed the flowers on the newspaper rack below the mailbox that hung to the right of the front door at eye level. There was no card, just the flowers.

~

It was a beautiful Easter Sunday morning, seventy-two degrees, but I could not see its beauty. All I knew was the hollow ache sitting in my chest. All I could think about was what happened on Good Friday. I replayed the events over and over in my mind, hoping each time that it was only a nightmare.

I called Dee after Mass. Her mother answered the phone and told me Dee was not home. I tried again before I left to return to school and got the same answer. I had my answer. It was over. To this day, I still get sad every Good Friday, and I think about Dee every twenty-seventh of September, her birthday.

I convinced Dee to go out with me a few times that summer after a considerable amount of begging but it was not the same. The girl who always sidled up to me in the car so quickly in the past suddenly was clutching the passenger side door handle as we drove to one of our old favorite places, the Raven Gallery in Southfield.

We'd always loved the folk music sounds of the sixties, the kind you could find in neighborhood coffee houses. That night, the music felt like it belonged to a different time, a different life.

The Raven Gallery was an intimate place, seating only about one hundred people at bistro-style tables, perfect for conversation between sets. The conversation that flowed so easily between us in the past was now strained. I was never the big conversationalist, preferring to hear the sparkle in her voice, but now I was carrying the bulk of the conversation. Her replies were limited to yes, no, or some other short answer. There was no smile in her voice and while most of the time she was staring out the window, I could detect no twinkle in her eyes when she was with me.

The air around her was different now—charged not with possibility but with exhaustion, as if she carried a secret gravity that repelled me gently, firmly, with every wordless silence. Each attempt at reconciliation became a rehearsal of surrender. I saw it in her posture: how she braced herself against the passenger-side door, fingers drumming lightly, gaze cast perpetually outward, seeking escape. Her voice was neutral, stripped of inflection, the musicality of their history reduced to a monotone. Even her laughter, once a bell in my chest, had gone underground.

I wondered if this was what adulthood felt like—a slow, relentless subtraction of innocence, each loss another notch in the soul. I told myself I would stop calling, that I would not write her letters, that I would let her go, but my hands betrayed me. Some nights I dialed her number just to hear the click of the rotary phone, a placeholder for the voice I missed. Each syllable of her absence became a lesson in restraint.

But even as hope shrank to a pinprick, something else grew in me, an awareness both ancient and new. I recalled long-ago lectures in the philosophy building, where a professor with an Old Testament beard had spoken of the highest forms of love—how agape, selfless love, is proved not in union but in relinquishment. The words had sounded abstract then, a trick of Christian dialectic meant to console the losers.

Now, sitting in the dark, I tasted their truth. No act would ever be more loving, more faithful to the spirit of our story, than to wish her happiness, even if it meant my own unhappiness. I felt it as a private vow, heavier and holier than any we had spoken under the stars of prom night or on the walk home after midnight Mass. I could not stop the ache, but I could choose its meaning.

The next day I went about my routine with mechanical diligence, each act a small petition to the universe for peace. I washed the family car, cut the grass with methodical stripes, each line a boundary between the before and after. In the evening, I took a long walk through the neighborhood—a territory haunted by the memory of her, but also, gradually, by something like acceptance. Families watered their lawns, porch lights clicked on, windows framed domestic scenes that seemed both unattainable and quietly reassuring. I realized that in order to honor what we had been; I had to stop trying to restore it, to resist the urge to unmake the break.

I tried seeing her a couple more times, knowing each time that it was fruitless. Clearly, there was no chance of reconciliation. I had a decision to make. I had long before reached that level of love that C. S. Lewis describes in his book "The Four Loves" as agape, an unconditional, selfless love. It was now time to test the unconditional nature of my love for her.

I could see that the only way to ensure my true love would be happy again was to give Dee her freedom—to allow her to love someone else. It was the hardest thing I have ever had to do in my life. What I wanted most out of life was not my happiness, but just to know that my love was truly happy.

As for me, the words of Kahlil Gibran describe it best "and ever has it been known that love knows not its own depth until the hour of separation."

I stopped calling.

CHAPTER 10

Philia Once Again

You are a whole that exists to live a life, not half a life
—Khalil Gibran

I plunged into a bottomless depression, my celebrated blue period. It was years before I was comfortable being around people again. I was so concerned that the least little thing, a familiar place, a remembered word or song on the radio would set me to crying again and I didn't want anyone to see that. I took different routes to places I had been with Dee—not because I planned to, but because I would find myself already turning before I knew why. At family dinners, I laughed at the right moments. I learned which questions to answer with a question.

My world narrowed to whatever was directly in front of me—a cup, a wall, a patch of floor—everything beyond that soft border gone unreliable and suspect.

I stopped reading faces. Other people's expressions seemed to carry too much, so I learned to look just past them, at the middle distance where nothing could catch me off guard.

Dee wrote me once a few months after the breakup, even though she told me she wouldn't. In the letter, she calmly explained her reasoning. It was a tender explanation. I kept the letter for years. After my tenth wedding anniversary, after I had three wonderful sons, I felt guilty for keeping the letter, so I threw it out. I kept only the last line, a line that summarized her reason for the breakup.

> Happiness comes of the capacity to feel deeply, to enjoy simply, to think freely, to risk life — to be needed

Even in her final words to me, Dee was still trying to teach me about love and life. I always thought the last words of her letter were profound and a fitting ending to our time together. I treasured them and what they represented—her final instructions as my teacher, my friend, my companion, my love.

Later in life, I discovered that the line was from a Storm Jameson quote. This underscored how well-read Dee was. Back then, one couldn't simply Google an appropriate quote; the research was more involved. I wish now that I had kept the letter.

The breakup was difficult, as I am sure it was for Dee. She no doubt took comfort in Mike's arms. How much she confided in him about me or the breakup, I cannot say. These things are never easy for either party. Dee and I spent nine hundred and thirty-five glorious days together, and I treasure the memory of every one. Still, for every day we shared, I spent three alone after that. Afraid to give myself to another, not trusting myself to love. There is no greater pain than the feeling of being completely alone. Yet I would not trade a single second of our time together to have avoided the difficult period that followed.

After a while, I tried dating again, but it was not the same. I did not have the strength of heart to go through another breakup. I became closed off, settling once again for Philia. Most of the women I dated after that eventually came to accept this part of me. One even asked me to be the best man at her wedding, which I gladly did. She was a good friend.

~

After graduating from college, I learned from my youngest sister that Dee was engaged. The family was all gathered around the dining room table, as we always did on Sundays and special occasions.

"Guess who I ran into today? Paulette. She told me that her sister Dee was engaged to be married." The cheerful lilt of my sister's voice struck me with violence, like a punch to my gut. It had been almost five years since Dee broke things off. Still, not a day went by that I didn't pray for reconciliation.

I choked on the piece of food I was chewing. Mom and my sisters looked up in unison at me. The last thing I wanted at that point was any attention. I swallowed the bit of dinner in my mouth, but completely lost my appetite. I excused myself from the table and took my plate to the kitchen sink.

Later, my sister asked, "Did anything that was said at dinner tonight upset you? Will you be alright?" She knew what was bothering me.

"I'll be okay. I just need to be alone for a while," I told her. When I heard the news for the first time that Dee was getting married, I couldn't help but think of the Jimmy Webb lyrics made popular by the

Brooklyn Bridge. Without a doubt, it was one of the worst days of my life.

I saw Dee at church one evening after that. We both still lived in Saint Suzanne's parish on the west side of Detroit. The hair was the same, that beautiful angelic face. Even the ring on her finger told me it was her. But she did not acknowledge my smiles or my attempts to get her attention from across the church.

~

I guess after college it was time for marriage. My neighbor and roommate freshman year, Jack, asked me to be his best man. He was marrying his high school sweetheart. Dee and I had double-dated often with Jack and Sue. I screwed up my courage and called Dee one last time. She was living in an apartment by then, but somehow I got her new phone number.

"Hi Dee, it's Wally."

"Oh, hi," came the reply. She did not sound happy to hear from me again.

"Hey, I know things are different between us and that we can never go back to being a couple, but Jack and Sue are getting married next Valentine's Day and I wanted to know if you would be my plus one. I understand we would go as just friends, but I thought you might like to see them again."

"Mmmm! Sure. I think that would be acceptable. Do you know where I live now?"

"No, not exactly. I just know you are not living at home."

She gave me her address, and I was all set. In my heart, I hoped we could get back together, but I knew that this was like winning the Mega Jackpot Lottery—fat chance.

Still, I sent her a bouquet to thank her for accepting my invitation. Being Valentine's Day and all, the florist told me they had only a limited selection of flowers that were uncommitted. I selected the cheapest one available, about a hundred dollars, and gave the florist the address. The note read, "Thank you for all you have given me, Wally."

When I came to pick up Dee at her apartment, it shocked me to see the flowers sitting on a table in her living room. There were at least three dozen red and white roses in a heart-shaped bouquet. The banner across the middle of the bouquet read "with all my love." When I saw the bouquet, I could only imagine what Dee must have thought when she first saw the flowers. I apologized, not wanting to offend her, and explained what the florist had told me and that it was my fault for failing to ask the florist to describe the flowers to me before I ordered them.

"I guess I would have been better off picking up three dozen dandelions, but I couldn't find any in February."

Dee smiled. I knew she would remember. And I knew she had forgiven me for the extravagant flowers.

We went to the wedding, and I had to sit at the main table with the rest of the wedding party, as I was the best man. I watched Dee the entire dinner, smiling at her, watching her talk to old friends we once shared. After the obligatory dance with the Maid-of-Honor and a quick dance with the bride, I danced the rest of the evening with Dee. I was grateful for the chance to be near her once more, even if it was as just a friend.

As we drove home, Dee got emotional; though she tried not to let me notice. We walked up to her apartment door in silence. When I turned to leave for the last time, she reached out and tenderly grabbed my arm.

"Friends can hug you know," she said.

I smiled. It was a thin, sad smile. I reached out and gave my dear, dear friend a tight embrace. I stroked her hair with my left hand one last time, patted her on the back with my right, kissed her on the cheek, repeatedly. She could still see the love in my eyes, feel it on her cheek, in the embrace's warmth.

~

A few days after the wedding, I received a letter. My heart leapt from my chest when I saw the handwriting on the envelope. I opened it quickly.

> Wally,
>
> It was especially good to see you again. We had such a fun time. It helped—it cleared up many misunderstandings. I still do care about you Wally, I always will. I wasn't lying when I said that there is a place that no one will ever be able to fill.
>
> It surprises me when you ask how I remember our years. It has been long, you know, and time has taken its course. Time has also been healing. I was so afraid for so long to show you or even to be honest enough with you to tell you that you are you—and that's special. But I wanted to mask those feelings for your sake because I thought you were still holding on. I didn't want to be misleading. Does that explain the bitter facade? They were happy—and we shared our first love together. I will never look back with remorse. How could I? The knowledge, the

sensitivity—it has all grown because of each other. I have learned and felt as much as you.

You will love again, Wally. Once you have loved, you will always love, and once you have been loved, you'll always need to be loved. It is a warmth that you have felt and never want to be without. I hope for you that the search will not be long.

I do not want you to feel that what we shared is minimized because of my involvement with Mike. It did happen quite quickly—but yet it was not without periods of thought about you.

Take care of yourself, please. And have a very happy birthday.

Tenderly,

dee

CHAPTER 11

Epilogue

You give but little when you give of your
possessions.
It is when you give of yourself that you truly
give.
—Khalil Gibran

The wedding gift felt heavy in my hands as I drove to her parents' house, an unannounced visit that was also an act of surrender. When Helen opened the door, the silence that met me said everything. We stood on the porch, two people who had once shared a kitchen and delightful conversation, now separated by a gift.

Included with the gift was a card. Inside was a handwritten note.

Mike,

You have been given the most precious gift a man could ever hope to receive, relayed through a simple word or a twinkle in an eye.

The fortune, bestowed upon you by the powers that be, has even greater significance when one stops to contemplate its source, for truly what greater gift might a man ask for? Not wealth for wealth is good only for a lifetime. Surely not fortune, for fortune is a fickle mistress, not even fame, for the heroes of today are buried tomorrow.

And yet all of these are yours, my friend, and so much more.

All is yours in the love of your wife.

Please love her and always be kind to her, for she deserves nothing less than everything.

Wally

I drove over to Saint Paul of the Cross Monastery the next day and parked my car right in back of the parking lot. At the time, I drove a flashy yellow two-seat sports car, a Pantera, which was hard to miss even if I tried to hide it. I was single and working a good job, so I had money and no one to spend it on. I parked at the far end of the lot and made my way to the Monastery.

I caught sight of Dee walking as if on a cloud towards the bridal ready room in the Monastery, a noticeable spring in her step as if to say that this was something she had been looking forward to for a long time and wanted to savor every step. Her head held high, a small, private smile on her lips.

She was radiant; dressed in white, and in place of a veil, she wore a white hooded cape. Sort of like a Little Red Riding Hood thing, except in white bridal silk. Even the angels wept at her beauty.

"Wally! I'm so glad you're here." A genuine, brilliant smile spread across her face. "I wanted you to see this. To see that I'm happy. Thank you for coming."

Dee kissed me on the cheek one last time.

I simply nodded and smiled. Seeing her in her wedding dress, that was all I could manage. I didn't trust my voice to say anything. I took her by both hands. Standing at arm's length, I spread her arms wide to drink in one last memory. She truly was happy, and that made it all right.

I turned to walk away from the chapel. I could not bear to watch the ceremony. For years afterwards, I could not listen to the Jim Webb song, "I heard you're getting married" without breaking down.

POSTSCRIPT

Memories

Your pain is the breaking of the shell that encloses your understanding.
—Khalil Gibran

That is my story, a story of the first love between a young girl and a young boy. It may not be the one you anticipated when you picked up this book. To be honest, it's not the one I intended to write when I set out on this journey with you, but first love is not always what you expect. Sometimes, as I'm beginning to understand as an author, the story you think you're telling turns out to be about something else entirely — and that something else is the thing that mattered all along.

First love is rarely neat. It is tangled in memories, threaded with both laughter and tears. And as Dee once said, the two people are always "young and stupid."

I will leave you with two quotes from Rod McKuen.

> I've been going a long time now
> Along the way I've learned some things.
> You have to make the good times yourself
> Take the little times and make them big times
> And save the times that are all right for the ones that
> aren't so good.

> It doesn't matter who you love, or how you love, but
> that you love.

ABOUT THE AUTHOR

W. M. J. Kreucher is a Detroit native with a passion for change. Over three decades, he made his mark in the automobile industry's environmental sector, ghostwriting for notable lawmakers and influencing key legislation. Now a fiction writer, he blends his rich experiences into stories that captivate and transport readers.

OTHER BOOKS BY THE AUTHOR

DANDELION MAN - THE FOUR LOVES

When a middle-aged man discovers his first love's father has died, he returns to Detroit after decades to confront the memory of the teenage romance that defined his understanding of love itself-only to discover that the past is never as finished as it seems.

PHARMACEUTICAL

When power corrupts, the truth becomes the ultimate prescription.

HEAVEN SENT

In the embrace of Michigan's woods, a journey of friendship, loss, and the blossoming of love.

THE INN AT HERON'S BAY

Whispers of history, echoes of love, and the secrets of a lost masterpiece—all in the tranquil embrace of Topsail's coast.

FOREVER AND A DAY

Sixty years of silence. One final chance to say goodbye.

DRONE

In the skies of power, a drone becomes the ultimate weapon.

AMIE

In the shadows of power, vengeance breeds a technological showdown.

TWO FOR VENGEANCE—THE KENNEDY CHRONICLES

DRONE and AMIE packaged in a single novel.

POLONIA—PANI DEWICKA AND OTHER STORIES

The challenges faced by an ethnic family that ultimately migrates to the United States.

THE BLUE NUN

From an ordinary life to a global terror plot, the unexpected journey of a mother and daughter unfolds.

WHILE DRIFTING SELECTED WORKS BY W. M. J. KREUCHER

Dandelion Man—the four loves, Pharmaceutical, Heaven Sent, The Inn at Heron's Bay, and Roses in December.

THE CURIOUS CASE OF THE BREVARD RECLUSE

In a town veiled by secrets, a child's discovery unravels a haunting mystery.

A PALLET OF DECEPTION

In the heart of a serene mountain town, one woman's passion for mystery could be the key to unveiling a deadly deception.

THE SECRETS OF EVERETT MANSION

Some secrets refuse to stay buried...

MURDER IN THE MOUNTAINS

When a famous documentarian is found dead at Looking Glass Falls, the Tuesday Night Book Club suspects foul play.